"So when do we start this . . . makeover?"
Edward asked.

"Tonight. The first thing we have to do is get you out of those clothes," Maribeth said.

"Hmmm. I like this already," he said, giving her a wicked grin. "Do you get to take yours off too?"

"Very funny," she muttered. "Now let's get started before you change your mind. First jeans, a couple of shirts, and boots."

"Never," he said firmly.

"Yes." Her mind was made up, and he couldn't change it. Before he knew what hit him, he stood before her in his new clothes. The denim molded to his thighs in a way that made Maribeth's mouth go dry. The shirt with pearl buttons fit him to a T and emphasized shoulders she was sure could support a porch swing. But it was the boots that produced the real transformation. His smile was brazen, his stance impudent and full of cocky male self-confidence. His message was clear. He wanted her. All she had to do was say when. . . .

WHAT ARE *LOVESWEPT* ROMANCES?

They are stories of true romance and touching emotion. We believe those two very important ingredients are constants in our highly sensual and very believable stories in the *LOVESWEPT* line. Our goal is to give you, the reader, stories of consistently high quality that may sometimes make you laugh, sometimes make you cry, but are always fresh and creative and contain many delightful surprises within their pages.

Most romance fans read an enormous number of books. Those they truly love, they keep. Others may be traded with friends and soon forgotten. We hope that each *LOVESWEPT* romance will be a treasure—a "keeper." We will always try to publish

*LOVE STORIES YOU'LL NEVER FORGET
BY AUTHORS YOU'LL ALWAYS REMEMBER*

The Editors

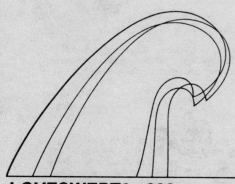

LOVESWEPT® • 220

Charlotte Hughes
Straight Shootin' Lady

BANTAM BOOKS
TORONTO • NEW YORK • LONDON • SYDNEY • AUCKLAND

STRAIGHT SHOOTIN' LADY

A Bantam Book / November 1987

LOVESWEPT® and the wave device are registered
trademarks of Bantam Books, Inc. Registered in U.S. Patent
and Trademark Office and elsewhere.

If you would be interested in receiving protective vinyl
covers for your Loveswept books, please write to this address
for information:

Loveswept
Bantam Books
P.O. Box 985
Hicksville, NY 11802

ISBN 0-553-21854-9

Published simultaneously in the United States and Canada

Bantam Books are published by Bantam Books, Inc. Its trademark, consisting of the words "Bantam Books" and the por-
trayal of a rooster, is Registered in U.S. Patent and Trademark
Office and in other countries. Marca Registrada. Bantam
Books, Inc., 666 Fifth Avenue, New York, New York 10103.

PRINTED IN THE UNITED STATES OF AMERICA

O   0 9 8 7 6 5 4 3 2 1

*To Barbara, who discovered
the writer in me and brought meaning
to my life*

One

Maribeth Bradford knew a suspicious face when she saw one. Having been the only child of a county sheriff and spending much of her twenty-four years listening to his tales, she couldn't help but recognize the signs. Her father had taught her what to look for in a potential crook, and the two men standing in the small old-fashioned lobby of the South Carolina State Bank definitely looked like a couple of shady characters. They were nervous, too, she noticed, as the man with thick horn-rimmed glasses shuffled from one foot to the other like a schoolboy who'd just been summoned to the principal's office. The other man—bald, heavyset, and wearing a light blue leisure suit—looked just as anxious as he stood at the marble customer counter in the center of the lobby and scribbled something on a piece of paper. Instinct told Maribeth he wasn't merely filling out a deposit slip. His other hand kept going to the side pocket of his jacket as though he were afraid something might fall out. Whatever it was, it created an untidy bulge in his pocket and was heavy enough to make his jacket hang unevenly. Was it a gun? she wondered. And that pillowcase. Were they planning to fill it with money?

They're going to rob the bank! she thought, coming wide-awake.

She almost dropped the clipboard that held the application she was filling out as a wave of panic washed over her. She glanced around frantically for Mr. Phelps, the security guard, who'd unlocked the front doors and let her in only moments before. He was standing at a teller's cage talking to a dark-haired man counting money. Even in her state of panic Maribeth did a double take on the handsome dark-haired man. He wasn't anybody she knew, she was sure. She would have remembered a face like that.

If only she could get his attention!

Remaining perfectly still on the leather sofa, she slid her hazel eyes from side to side, trying to get a better grip on the situation. She tilted her head forward slightly as she did so, letting her blond hair form a curtain on either side of her face so the robbers wouldn't notice her anxious perusings and suspect she was on to them. There were only about eight bank employees present, Maribeth noted, each in the task of opening for business. Thankfully the customers hadn't started coming in yet. There were offices in back, she knew, but a wall separated them from the lobby, so there was no way of knowing how many people were there.

She waited another second, but when neither the security guard nor the other man looked up from the teller window, she knew it was up to her. She tightened her grip on the clipboard, grasping it as though it were a lifeline and she a drowning woman. She glanced in the direction of the dubious looking twosome and turned away quickly when the man with glasses looked up and caught her staring. He frowned and nudged his friend.

Keeping her eyes straight ahead, Maribeth pried her

ramrod body from the sofa and walked slowly in the direction of the tellers' windows. There were six of them, each with iron bars bolted to a long marble counter that matched the highly polished floors. The bank looked much the same as it had when she'd first seen it as a little girl. The only thing missing was the antique brass birdcage filled with parakeets that had stood in the lobby for as long as she could remember, but she didn't have time to worry about that at the moment. She was almost there, only inches from the window where the guard stood. She didn't hear the man come up behind her.

"Freeze, lady," a menacing voice said at her ear.

Maribeth whirled around and flashed the bald man a dazzling smile. "Oh, did I steal your place in line?" she asked in mock innocence.

"Shut up!" the man barked nervously, and jabbed a pistol against her ribs. Several tellers gasped, and one woman screamed as the man counting money looked up in surprise. The guard reached for his gun.

"I wouldn't do that, old fella," the man holding the gun on Maribeth warned, "unless you want to make funeral arrangements for this little lady." The guard moved his hand away from the gun instantly.

"Okay, everybody put your hands high in the air," the thug said, the barrel of his pistol still pressed against Maribeth's rib cage. He glanced over at his partner, the man with thick glasses. "Joe, get the guard's gun."

The man blinked. "My name's not Joe."

The bald, heavyset robber rolled his eyes and muttered a curse that only Maribeth could hear. "You wanna use our real names, stupid?"

"Yeah, right," the man with the horn-rims said, nodding. "I see what you mean." He started for the guard and stopped. "Uh, what am I supposed to call you?"

The robber sighed heavily, giving his partner a look

of pure exasperation. "I don't give a damn *what* you call me. Just get the guard's gun, for crying out loud! And search his friend while you're at it."

"I'll call you Barney," the man given the name Joe said, and hurried through the saloon-style doors that separated the lobby from the teller work area.

Maribeth watched Joe frisk Mr. Phelps, taking his gun, and then frisk the younger man. The latter scowled darkly, and she wondered how he could look so handsome one minute and so deadly the next. He made Joe nervous, she noticed, watching the crook tremble as he checked the man for possible arms.

"Now," Barney said, "lock all the doors and search the offices in back . . . and the bathrooms too." He gave Maribeth a lopsided smile, showing crooked yellow teeth. "We don't want nobody to miss the party now, do we?" She wrinkled her nose at him in distaste, and he laughed.

Joe returned empty-handed. "All the doors are locked, and it's all clear in back."

"Good. Now, round everybody up and search 'em for weapons."

Joe busied himself doing as he was told. "Everybody's clean," he announced as soon as he was finished.

Barney nodded his approval. "Now, move 'em into one of those back offices and tie 'em up. Use the cords on the drapes if you have to. You, too, handsome," he said to the dark-headed man next to the security guard.

Although the guard moved dutifully toward the group of people, the younger man didn't budge. "I'm an employee of the bank," he said. "Let the woman go, and I'll give you whatever you want."

Maribeth raised her eyes to his face. He was even nicer-looking up close, she thought. His eyes were the same rich shade of brown as his hair. His nose was a bit large, she noticed, but added strength and character to an otherwise perfect set of features. And his clothes. Even with her lack of experience in buying expensive clothes, she could tell his suit was custom-tailored and had probably cost a small fortune. It made her corduroy skirt and jacket look tacky by comparison. But with the March temperatures being cooler than usual, it was the best outfit she owned. Oh, for goodness' sake, she thought. Here she was ogling some man when she was about to be blown to smithereens!

"We're giving the orders here, chump," Barney said. "If you want to live to see Christmas, you'd better do as you're told."

The banker glanced at Maribeth. Their eyes locked briefly, and she thought she detected some emotion there. Was it pity?

"I told you to let the woman go and I would cooperate," he insisted.

Barney studied him for a moment. "What's your name, fancy pants?" he asked, suddenly interested in the man.

"Edward."

"And your position?"

"I'm a clerk."

"Pretty fancy clothes for a clerk," Barney said, taking in his attire.

Edward shrugged. "When you own only one suit, you can afford the best."

Barney laughed and glanced over at his partner. "Throw fancy pants that pillowcase," he said. "I'll work on getting the money while you tie up these people." Joe tossed Edward the pillowcase and ordered the group of people, including the guard, into a straight line and moved them single file through the doorway to the back offices.

"Well, don't just stand there," Barney snapped at Edward. "Fill the bag with money!" He motioned to the cash drawer with his gun.

Maribeth watched Edward move with deliberate slowness and wondered if he was trying to buy time or merely intimidate the robber, or both. "Do you want this in small or large bills?" Edward asked.

Veins popped out at Barney's temples, and it was obvious he was at the boiling point. "I want it all, buster," he said. "I want what's in those drawers, and I want what's in that vault. Now, stop stalling!"

"I can't open the vault," Edward said calmly.

Maribeth froze. This was it, she thought, preparing to die.

Barney stared at Edward for a full minute, his face turning an ugly shade of red. "What the hell do you mean, you can't open the vault?"

"I don't have the combination. The president of the bank is the only one who knows it, and he's not here."

"And just where might he be?" Barney asked, obviously becoming more angry and irritated by the minute.

"He left for an appointment right after we opened. As a matter of fact, you just missed him. I don't expect him back until after lunch."

Barney slammed his fist on the marble counter, then winced from the excruciating pain. "This better be for real, fancy pants, or I'm gonna—" His threat was cut short by the sound of a police siren. He mouthed off a list of obscenities that made Maribeth shudder. "Okay, who's the wise guy who called the cops?" he asked, looking directly at Edward. He grabbed Maribeth around the neck, and when it looked like Edward might make a move, he shoved the pistol against her skull. "Just try it, mister, and this lady bites the dust." The threat worked. Edward stopped dead in his tracks.

Joe rushed through the door. "What are we going to do now?" he asked in a panicky voice. "The cops—"

"They ain't gonna do nothing," Barney snapped, still pointing the gun at Maribeth's head. "If they so much as come near this place, I'm gonna give it to Goldilocks here."

Maribeth closed her eyes. This was it, she told herself once again.

"I see you get your thrills scaring innocent women," Edward said caustically. "What do you do for an encore? Kick small animals?"

Barney glared at him. "No, but I'd get a thrill shooting you, buster. Now keep quiet." He looked at his partner. "Is everybody tied up?"

Joe nodded. "Tight as a drum."

"Good. Now, you stay out here and make sure fancy pants puts all the money in the bag. Me and cutie-pie are goin' in the back. Move it, sister," he ordered tersely.

Maribeth opened her eyes and gave her captor a dirty look. If he was going to shoot her, he'd shoot her. But she wasn't about to let him think she was afraid of him.

"Hey, what are you gonna do?" Joe asked nervously.

"I'm gonna find us a nice office to hole up in till I figure out our next move." He guided Maribeth toward the back of the lobby, where the doors led to the hallway. "When handsome finishes filling that pillowcase, bring him with you. And keep your gun on him. He's feisty." Barney nudged Maribeth through the door and into the hallway. They passed the office where the employees were being held. At the end of the hall he shoved her through the door into a small office containing only a desk and a couple of chairs. On the other side of the room was another door that led into a much larger office. "James E. Spears, President," he said, reading the gold engraving on the heavy wooden door. "I reckon this office is good enough. What d'you think, blondie?"

Maribeth glared at him as she walked into the impressive office. A mahogany desk dominated the room, and behind it was a credenza of the same rich wood grain. The chairs and couch surrounding it were of fine leather in a burgundy color. She glanced over her shoulder, wishing Edward would join her, but she saw she and Barney were alone. She was worried about Edward, the way he was mouthing off at the robbers. He could end up getting shot if he wasn't careful. She sighed. Well, she was going to have to prevent it somehow. Barney motioned for her to take a seat and she did. It was time to come up with a plan.

"What do you mean, you can't open the vault?" Joe asked, echoing his partner's previous words.

Edward sighed, holding the half-filled pillowcase in one hand. "The president of the bank is the only one who knows the combination. I've already explained that to your partner." A sheriff's car careened around a corner and came to an abrupt halt in front of the bank. Joe darted behind a file cabinet, his gun still poised at Edward. Several other patrol cars slid into place beside the first one. Sirens squealed loudly, and blue lights flashed from each car, making the parking area look like an amusement park. Edward glanced at the man. He looked pathetic crouched behind the cabinet like a frightened animal. "You could surrender, you know," he said, but his mind wasn't really on Joe. He was more concerned about the girl. If that crook did so much as touch her . . .

"Yeah, and have my head blown off in the process," Joe answered. "How much we got in the bag?"

"Thirty or forty thousand."

"Ah, damn!" Joe muttered. "Barney is going to have a fit when he finds out we went to this much trouble for a lousy thirty or forty grand."

"Not worth going to prison over, is it?"

"Save your speeches," Joe said angrily. "I ain't interested. Barney will know what to do."

• • •

". . . and I have these two cats, Corn Flake and Raisin Bran," Maribeth continued. "I named them that because one looked like a shriveled-up raisin when she was born, and the other is the color of Corn Flakes—and they need to be fed twice a day. If you kill me, they're likely to starve before anyone finds them. Of course, if my landlady finds out I have cats, she's going to evict me. I'm not supposed to have them, y'see," she explained, without stopping for breath. "Not that it'll matter if I'm dead, mind you, but I just moved into that apartment, and I don't want to have to move again. I was living in Atlanta with my best friend until she—"

"Would you shut up!" Barney bellowed, pressing his fingers to his temples as though in great pain. "I ain't interested in your stupid cats *or* your apartment *or* your best friend."

Maribeth gave him a hateful look. "Well, you don't have to be so rude, you know. I've done everything you've told me."

"Except close your big mouth."

"I don't know why you're holding me," she continued. "Nobody is going to ransom me, if that's what you think. I don't know anybody with that kind of money. I *do* have forty-seven dollars hidden under my mattress at home that you're welcome to."

"Under your mattress?"

"Uh-huh. That's where I keep my money. I don't trust banks; you never know what might happen. But I guess I don't have to tell *you* that."

Barney scowled. "This is the last time I'm going to tell you to shut up." He pulled a stained handkerchief from his pocket. "See this? If I have to tell you again, I'm going to gag you."

"You're not putting that filthy thing in my mouth," Maribeth said.

"Filthy! I'll have you know I washed these clothes yesterday."

"Then you must've slept in a barn last night, because you smell like something I once stepped in at my uncle's farm."

"You've got a smart-aleck mouth on you, you know that?" Barney said. "Why, if I was your pa, which I'm glad I ain't, I would—" He was interrupted by Joe's appearance.

"This place is crawling with cops," he sputtered, nudging Edward through the doorway with his gun.

"Did ya get the money?"

"Part of it." He glanced at Edward. "Except what's in the vault."

Maribeth gazed at Edward, thankful he was unharmed. She noticed he was staring at her as well, and the expression in his eyes bordered on tenderness. She was the first to look away.

"You'd better not be lying to us about that vault, handsome," Barney said, "or you and the girl will pay. Now, get on that telephone and call the Sheriff's Department and give 'em our demands."

Edward sighed as he picked up the telephone. "Okay, what are they?"

"One million dollars and a private plane out of here."

Edward laughed. "You must be kidding. You aren't going to find that kind of money in this town."

Barney buried his face in his hands, giving an enormous sigh of frustration. He looked at Joe. "I told you we shouldn't have tried to rob this hick town." He turned back to Edward. "Okay, five hundred thousand. Not a penny less. And don't forget to tell 'em we got hostages."

Edward dialed the emergency number and was put through to the sheriff right away. He hung up several minutes later after relaying the demands. "He said he'll work on it and get back to us."

Barney gave him a yellow-toothed grin. "I knew they'd cooperate. Joe, cut the cords on the drapes and tie these two up," he said, motioning to Maribeth and Edward. "Stick 'em in the closet."

"You can't be serious!" Maribeth cried in disbelief.

"And stuff something in her mouth so she'll shut up," he added. "That's the noisiest broad I've ever had the misfortune to run into."

"I don't appreciate the way you're treating us," Maribeth said in a huff. "Especially after I offered you every dime I had. Furthermore, when my father hears about this, he'll hunt you down and—" She was prevented from saying anything further when Joe shoved her toward the closet.

Joe placed them back-to-back in the closet and tied their hands together. When he had tied the last knot, he gave Maribeth a look of warning. "Now, keep quiet or I'll gag you." Maribeth stuck her tongue out at him.

"Are you okay?" Edward asked as soon as Joe had closed the door.

"I guess," she muttered. She struggled with the ropes but realized it was useless. She gritted her teeth. The nerve of those two!

"Don't do that," Edward said. "You'll only make the knots tighter."

"What do you expect me to do? Just sit here?"

"For the time being. But I have a plan."

"You do?" She perked up instantly.

"Yeah. they want an airplane, right? I'll bet neither of them has the slightest idea how to fly one. But I do. I'm going to offer to fly them out of here if they let everybody go."

"But what about you?"

"They won't hurt me. As long as I fly them where they want to go."

His voice was strong and confident and reassuring, but still . . . "I don't know, Edward," she said, liking the sound of his name on her tongue. "That one named Barney looks awfully mean. Besides, it could take all day to get that kind of money, as well as a plane. We could still be sitting here this time tomorrow." She sighed heavily. "My poor cats. I should never have come back to this town. Who would ever suspect that anyone would try to rob a dinky little bank in Laurel, South Carolina?"

"I don't think it's dinky," Edward said defensively.

"It's all my fault," she said, sighing. "I'm jinxed."

Edward laughed softly. "I doubt that," he said, wondering what kind of perfume she wore. It wasn't sickly-sweet like the scent some of the older women in town wore, and the fragrance didn't smother him. Instead, he caught the occasional whiff of something pleasant. It made him think of spring.

"No, truly I am," she insisted. "I've been jinxed for weeks now. First, my best friend decides to marry a man she's known less than two weeks, and she moves out on me. Just like that. Then, because I can't afford the rent, I start interviewing for a better-paying job and what happens?" She didn't wait for him to answer. "My boss finds out and fires me. So I decide to move back to Laurel, because I wasn't all that crazy about living in a big city in the first place—which, I might add, cost me every cent I had—but when I come here to apply for a job, I get stuck right smack in the middle of a bank robbery!"

Edward felt the corners of his lips tug into a smile. The poor girl was really having a tough time, and he ached to put his arm around her. He was determined to get them out of their present predicament. "What kind of position are you looking for?" he asked. Perhaps if he kept her talking, she'd be less afraid.

"I was applying for the administrative assistant's job," she said, "reporting to the president. Of course, I'll never get it."

"Why not?"

"I don't meet all the qualifications. For instance, he

wants someone who takes shorthand. I wouldn't know shorthand from Braille. I doubt I'd get along with him anyway. He's probably the stuffed-shirt type. He's a New Yorker, I hear; a big-city banker. Why he decided to come to a small town like this is beyond me. He'll never make it. I bet he expects his assistant to bring him coffee every time his cup runs low, and run his personal errands as well as keep up with his wife's birthday."

"I happen to know he's not married."

"Probably because nobody will have him." She shrugged. "Anyway, people say he's nothing like his grandfather, who ran the bank for forty years before he died. And Sara Rawlings, who knows everybody's business, says he came here straight from Wall Street."

A half smile, half frown, played across Edward's lips. He liked the feel of her against him, the way her hair tickled the back of his neck when she moved her head. Her hair was one of the first things he'd noticed about her, thick blond curls cascading down graceful shoulders. And her eyes. He was sure they were blue. Or were they green? They seemed to change when the light hit them a certain way. He realized suddenly she had asked a question. "I'm sorry," he said. "What did you say?"

"I was just wondering what you thought of Mr. Spears," she said. Actually she was more interested in the man she was tied to. His back felt broad and strong, and for some reason his presence made her less afraid.

"Well . . ." Edward knew he was in a bad predicament. "He's a nice guy and all and he's fair enough with his employees."

"Does he pay well?"

"Yes, that's one thing I can vouch for. He pays very well."

Maribeth sighed. "There aren't many jobs in this town, as you probably already know, and most of them don't pay worth a flip." She paused. "I suppose I could lie about my qualifications, just to prove I could do the job," She sighed again. "But I've never been good at lying. I might as well have Pinocchio's nose when it comes to fibbing."

"Why would you want a job you're not qualified for?"

"I said I didn't meet *his* qualifications," she said indignantly. "That doesn't mean I can't do the job." Maribeth had been straining, trying not to let her fingers touch his, but it was almost impossible with their wrists tied together as they were. She relaxed her shoulders and arms, as well as her fingers, all of which had grown sore and stiff. Her fingers brushed his and she tensed slightly wondering if he'd noticed. His hands were big and warm and comforting as she let her smaller ones rest against his open palm. She couldn't help but wonder if he was married, but she knew there was no way to find out without being obvious.

Probably has a wife and six kids, she thought glumly.

"How much longer do you think they're going to keep us tied up?" she asked, suddenly impatient to get out of the small closet. Inhaling Edward's after-shave was proving hazardous to her senses.

"I'm sure the Sheriff's Department is working as quickly as they can."

"Well, I don't have all day," she said irritably. "I've got a million things to do back at my apartment, what with moving in and all." She sighed. "And I've got to look for a job." She struggled against the cord once more in vain. Her entire body was sore from being scrunched up so long. She leaned against the door and began banging on it with her elbow.

"What are you doing?"

"Trying to get us out of this stupid closet," she said, wondering if her half-cocked plan would work. "Hello, out there," she called loudly. "Can you guys hear me?"

She sighed. Where were bank robbers when you really needed them?

"Don't try anything," Edward warned.

Joe jerked the door open. "I should have known you couldn't keep quiet for long."

"I have to go to the bathroom."

"Hold it."

"I *have* been holding it," she said in a deliberately petulant voice.

"Oh, for heaven's sake," Joe muttered. "Why didn't you say something before I went to all the trouble of tying you up?"

"I didn't have to go then," she said, her voice becoming saccharine-sweet. She hoped the slight quaver didn't give her away. She was beginning to tremble, and a knot of fear was growing in her stomach, reminding her what she was about to do was dangerous. They could be killed.

From her vantage point Maribeth could see that Barney was resting his head against the back of the chair, both feet propped on the desk. Although he held the gun in his hand, his arms were crossed, and he seemed to be in a relaxed state. It would take at least two seconds for him to shoot, maybe three, Maribeth figured. She would have to beat him to it.

Joe worked at untying the knots as best he could with one hand. Then, frustrated, he muttered an oath and laid his gun aside. Maribeth felt the cords loosen around her wrists and stifled the urge to pounce on the gun. She waited patiently for Joe to finish untying her completely as she gauged the distance. Two seconds was all she would have, three at the most. One slip could prove fatal for Edward and her. She frowned. The thought of Edward being shot was not a pleasant one. He was sitting very still behind her, as though he sensed something was about to happen.

Maribeth could feel the heavy thud of her heart and

was certain everyone in the room heard it. Joe pulled the last of the knots free and turned toward his gun. Maribeth sprang forward. She was faster.

"Hey, what the—" Joe barely had time to utter the words before Barney leaped from the desk and aimed his gun with the speed and agility of a man half his age. Maribeth, too, aimed with split-second precision.

The shot was deafening, followed by the acrid smell of gunpowder. Shock rendered them all motionless for a second, then Barney dropped his gaze to his hand. The pistol fell to the floor.

"She shot me!" he cried in horror. "That loudmouthed broad shot me!"

Maribeth raised herself slowly from the floor, the gun poised in midair, her eyes darting from one robber to the other. "I only nicked you," she said. "But if you make a move for that gun, I'm going to bury the next bullet so deep, they'll never find it." Her voice sounded sure and authoritative in her own ears. Inside her stomach was flip-flopping like a wet fish just thrown to shore. She could hear her father's voice. "Look them straight in the eye, Maribeth. Never let on like you're afraid."

Neither Joe nor Barney budged as she claimed the other gun. She aimed it directly at Joe, who cowered against the wall. "Untie Edward," she ordered, gripping both pistols so tight, it hurt. She took a deep breath. Lord, please don't let my legs give out now, she prayed silently. Shooting at targets and old tin cans was a whole lot different from confronting bank robbers.

She waited until Edward joined her before handing him both guns. He hesitated. "I need to wrap Barney's hand," she said, seeing the question in his eyes. "If either of them moves, shoot."

Edward was still staring in awe when she finished wrapping Barney's hand in his own dirty handkerchief. "Where did you learn to shoot like that?" he asked.

"My father taught me."

"Your father? Is he a gunslinger?"

"He used to be the county sheriff here. He's retired now. Are you okay?"

Edward nodded. "And you?" His gaze traveled the length of her, and she felt her body tingle in response as she nodded too. "I guess we need to check the others," he said.

"I guess." She didn't want to leave him right now, but she knew she had to. "Do you want to let the deputies in or should I?"

"I'll do it," he said, gladly handing over the pistols. He wasn't about to confess he hadn't the slightest idea how to use one. He glanced at the robbers, then back to her. "I need to tell you something," he said hesitantly. "I wanted to tell you sooner, but I was afraid those two would hear and take advantage of the situation."

Maribeth raised both brows. She couldn't imagine what was so important they had to keep the sheriff waiting. "What is it?"

"I'm James E. Spears."

She blinked. "Who?"

"The president of the bank. The *E* stands for Edward." He gave her an apologetic smile. "If those two had known who I was, I'm afraid I would have had no choice but to open the vault."

"Oh." She sighed heavily. "Well, I did it again. Put both feet in my mouth. It happens all the time. I often wonder why I don't just have my jaw wired shut permanently."

Edward grinned. "Yes, you do have quite a mouth on you, don't you? But I think that's one of the reasons I like you and want to hire you."

Her jaw dropped in disbelief. "You want to hire me? After all I said?"

He chuckled at her outright shock. "As soon as you tell me your name. Unless you'd rather I just call you Gunsmoke."

"Maribeth Bradford," she mumbled.

He liked it. It sounded straightforward and down-to-earth like her. "Okay, Maribeth Bradford. The job is yours if you want it."

"But I'm not qualified."

"That's not what you said in the closet a few minutes ago."

Her gaze dropped from his eyes to his smiling mouth. His teeth were white and straight as a yardstick. He'd be wonderful in toothpaste commercials, Maribeth thought. Lord, how would she ever work for him? "Why are you doing this?" she asked.

He didn't hesitate. "Because you impress the hell out of me," he said, his expression sobering. "What you did just now took a lot of guts." He paused briefly. "And we both know the people in this town are having a hard time accepting a new face in the bank. With your help—" He didn't finish the sentence. "What do you say?"

She would never be able to work for him. "When would you need me to start?"

"Tomorrow."

Maybe if he toned down the after-shave. "Tomorrow?"

"We open at nine o'clock sharp."

They would be working in completely different rooms; she wouldn't have to sit right next to him. "Nine?"

"Do you always repeat everything someone else says?"

She blushed. "Only when I lack for words."

"Which isn't often, I'll bet. I need your answer, Maribeth. There are people tied up in the next room and deputies lining the street and—"

"I'll do it," she announced quickly. She had to have a job, didn't she?

He rewarded her with a smile. "Good." He started to move away, then stopped abruptly. "By the way." He leaned close to her, his face only inches from hers, so close that when he spoke, his breath fanned her cheeks with a clean warm scent. "You won't have to run any errands for me, Maribeth. When I buy gifts for my woman, I like to select each item personally." He winked at her once and was gone.

Two

Maribeth's car slid across the gravel parking lot, kicking up dust and pebbles in its wake. She shoved the gears into park and checked her wristwatch. Nine-fifteen. Of all times for her alarm clock to go on the blink! Quickly she plucked the remaining hot curlers from her hair and tossed them onto the seat where the others lay. She found her hairbrush and pulled it through her thick hair, trying to bring some kind of order to her appearance. Someone called her name and she glanced up. Carol McCloy, another bank employee, hurried toward her.

"Carol, hi," Maribeth said, climbing out of the car. Carol had changed very little since their high school days. She wore her strawberry-blond hair in the same pageboy that had been so fashionable back then, and her petite figure was still very attractive. Carol had recently married Dan McCloy, who'd just opened Dan's Carpets, and it was no secret they hoped to start their family soon.

"I see you're late too," Carol said, trying to keep up with Maribeth's long-legged stride.

"Yes, and on my first day! I wonder if Mr. Spears has ever fired anyone on their first day."

Carol laughed. "I doubt he'll fire you just for being late. Not after what you did yesterday." Carol had been among the group of people tied up in the back office. "Did you know the robbery attempt made all the papers?" she asked. "They're calling you a heroine. And your picture was on the eleven o'clock news."

"I didn't see it," Maribeth confessed, somewhat flattered. "I went to bed early."

"All that excitement wear you out?"

She laughed. "I guess so." They had reached the entrance to the bank, and she opened the door and motioned for Carol to pass through first. "I must've answered at least a hundred questions from dozens of reporters."

"What was it like being tied to Mr. Spears in a dark closet?" Carol whispered.

"I can't remember," Maribeth lied. "I was too scared."

"You've always had more guts than the rest of us," Carol said. "Must've gotten it from your father. By the way"—she paused and glanced at Maribeth—"have you seen Moss since you got back?"

Maribeth had known the question was coming. Sooner or later someone was going to ask her about Moss Gentry. Even so, she wasn't prepared. "The last time I saw Moss, he said he never wanted to lay eyes on me again."

Carol laughed. "That's only because you decided to run off to Atlanta with Peg instead of marrying him like he wanted."

"That was a long time ago. I'm sure Moss understands now why I had to leave. There could never be anything between us."

Carol didn't press her. "Is that your lunch you're carrying?"

"Uh-huh." Maribeth glanced down at the small brown

bag in her hand. She wasn't about to admit she couldn't afford to buy her lunch.

"I brought mine too. Why don't we have lunch together in the square?"

"Okay. But right now I'd better find my desk before Mr. Spears hires a replacement." She cleared the lobby in record time and hurried through the doors that led to the back offices.

It all looked different today, thank goodness, but she couldn't suppress the shudder as she remembered what had taken place the day before.

She found her office, the small one that led into Edward's. The first thing she noticed was a large pot of fresh flowers on her desk. She picked up the card bearing the name of the local florist and opened it. *Welcome home. Love, Moss.* She stared at the card for a minute, trying to read between the lines. Did this mean they were friends again?

She tucked the card into the top drawer of her desk and was just about to sit down when she heard a woman's voice, loud and high-pitched, coming from Edward's office. The door opened abruptly and an elderly woman stalked out. Maribeth recognized seventy-year-old Gertrude Givens immediately.

She was livid.

"Maribeth!" Gertrude hurried toward her, shaking a stack of papers in her face. "Do you know the meaning of this?" Edward Spears was right behind her.

Maribeth glanced at him briefly before taking the papers from Gertrude. "It looks like a loan application."

"Of course, it's a loan application," Gertrude said, snatching the papers away. "Any fool can see that. But can you believe this man expects me to fill these out before I can have any money?" She gave Edward a withering look. "I've been coming to this bank for almost thirty years, and I've *never* had to fill out any forms. If I needed money for my nursery supplies, James just handed it over, and I would pay him back at the end of the season. But this young whippersnapper—" She gave a huff of pure disgust.

"I've already explained the policies," Edward said. His tone was polite and professional. "all I need is your signature and what collateral you have to offer—"

"Collateral!" Gertrude pulled herself up to her full height, which couldn't have been more than five feet. "I'll tell you what collateral I have, young man. I have my word as an honest and respectable citizen of this town. If that's not good enough—"

"I never said that, Miss Givens," he said patiently, "but you'll have to understand we have rules and regulations we must follow."

Gertrude snorted. "Rules shmules. You and your rules can go back to Wall Street, Mr. Spears. Now, if you'll excuse me, I think I'll take my business elsewhere." She was gone before anyone could stop her.

Maribeth and Edward merely stared at the empty doorway for a moment. "Welcome to the banking industry, Gunsmoke," he said wryly.

She shook her head. "Oh, Mr. Spears—"

"Edward," he said. "I think after what we went through yesterday, we can at least be on a first-name basis."

She nodded absently, but her mind was on Gertrude. "I don't think I've ever seen Miss Givens so angry," she said. "I know she has a bad temper and all, and that she's difficult at times."

"Calling Miss Givens's disposition difficult is like saying Moby Dick was a big fish," he said dryly. "She was mad when she came in here, telling me I had no right to remove my grandfather's parakeets, said they were as much a part of the bank as he was."

"Yes, I noticed yesterday the cage was gone. Why did you get rid of it?" She watched him move to her desk and sit on the edge, taking care not to upset the pot of flowers.

"The cleaning lady kept complaining about the mess. The birds kicked seed all over the floor. And frankly they smelled.

"Anyway," he continued, "Miss Givens went on to tell me how wonderful the bank was when my grandfather ran it, almost as though it were my fault the man died in the first place. When I pulled out one of those loan applications, she hit the ceiling."

Maribeth tried not to notice how nicely his pants stretched across his lean thighs. He looked clean and fresh and smelled of soap and after-shave. "Where did you get those forms in the first place?" she asked, noting the odd pitch in her voice.

"I found them near the birdcage. I think my grandfather used them to line the bottom of the cage. Can you believe it?"

"Edward—" She paused. He might not appreciate her butting in. "You're not going to be able to walk into this bank and change everything overnight. People won't like it."

"You mean, because I removed a smelly birdcage, for heaven's sake?"

"Not only that, but Miss Givens shouldn't have to go through such a fuss over a simple loan. She was a customer in this bank long before I was born. She and your grandfather had their own way of doing business."

"There's only one problem with that," he said. "Before today I never saw the lady in my life, and where I come from we use loan applications and discuss collateral."

"This isn't New York City," she reminded him. "We do things differently."

"I'm well aware of that," he said, "but business is business, Maribeth."

Maribeth bit back a retort. After all, he *was* her boss and she needed the job. Perhaps she should approach him from another angle. "Okay," she said, as a thought hit her. "We could draw up two loan application forms, a long form for people we don't know and a short one for those we *do* know." Her grin was impish. "After all, the IRS has a long and short form. Why can't we?"

Her smile warmed him, and he felt his own lips tug at the corners. "There's only one problem with that, Gunsmoke. I only know about three people in town, including you." His eyes were on her hair as he spoke. Nice hair, he thought. He had an urge to brush one fat curl across his lips. "How are you today?" he asked, changing the subject. He suddenly realized he had no desire to argue with her.

"Fine."

"No aftershocks from yesterday?"

She shook her head. "I slept like a baby last night."

Edward took a deep breath. Why was his overactive mind conjuring up all kinds of images of her in bed? He didn't have to have a good imagination to know she would be soft and silky smooth, and warm as a kitten. He cleared his throat in an attempt to clear his head. "By the way, the mayor's office called. He wants to have a luncheon in your honor. For stopping the robbery."

She blushed. "He doesn't have to do that."

"And some guy named Moss called twice, said he wanted to make sure you were all right after yesterday. I assured him you were, although he didn't sound like he wanted to take my word for it. Is he a boyfriend?" He knew he was being personal but couldn't help it.

"No," she said, glancing at the flowers. "Just an old friend."

Edward knew then who'd sent them. "I suppose I should thank you for saving my life."

Her eyes crept slowly to his face. The look there was startlingly tender. "I really didn't do all that much," she said, praying that her fluttering heart would not suddenly burst from her chest in flight.

"My mother would not agree with you," he said, smiling.

His smile was totally disarming, and Maribeth had the strange urge to run her finger across the upper lip where it curled captivatingly. She put her hands together nervously and found them damp. "I suppose I should get to work," she said, trying to sound professional, at the same time wondering if anyone was going to train her. Something told her she was going to have to jump right in and figure it all out for herself.

She walked around her desk and sat down, trying to look cool and composed. She saw the stack of papers beside her typewriter and sighed in relief at having found something to do. "I suppose you want these typed," she said.

"Would you like me to explain any of it to you?" he asked politely.

"That won't be necessary," she said. "You just go on with whatever it is you do around here. I'll manage perfectly."

He stood and stretched. "Well, I suppose I should go into my office and think up new ways to lose customers."

Where was the stupid switch that turned on the blasted typewriter! Maribeth wondered. She tried to search for it without being obvious. "Yes, well, you certainly seem to be doing a good job of that," she said, not really paying attention to the conversation. She didn't see the dark look he gave her as he walked into his office.

The telephone rang, and Maribeth picked it up and answered in her most professional voice. She'd show smarty britches just how good she was. "Oh, hello, Moss," she said, recognizing the voice on the other end instantly.

"It's been a long time, Maribeth."

"Moss, I can't talk now," she whispered. The last thing she needed at the moment was a personal phone call. Things weren't going well as it was.

"When can I see you?"

She tapped her fingers nervously against the phone. "Oh, whenever," she said vaguely. "I have to go now."

Maribeth hung up. What could Moss Gentry possibly have to say to her after all this time? Was he still angry? She hoped not. She didn't want to see a twenty-year-old relationship thrown away. Perhaps he'd come to terms with that relationship and now saw it for what it was—friendship and nothing more. She glanced at the flowers and realized she'd forgotten to thank him. No doubt she'd have the opportunity before long. She was already dreading it.

"People are complaining," Maribeth said a few days later, standing at the door to Edward's office.

He looked up from his work and motioned for her to take a seat in one of the chairs in front of his desk. He watched her walk toward the chair with the grace of a queen and couldn't believe she was the same woman he'd seen wielding a six-shooter less than a week before. "What is it this time?"

Maribeth came straight to the point. "They're complaining because you removed the coffee and donuts from the lobby."

Edward leaned back in his chair and sighed. It was hard to believe he'd once made monumental decisions on Wall Street. Now, his problems centered on parakeets' cages, what color to paint the bathrooms, and whether or not to serve coffee and donuts to his customers.

"Maribeth, this is a bank, not a coffee shop. Besides, we were wasting more than people were eating."

"I know that. But your grandfather did it for years . . ."

"Here we go again," he said dully.

"He said it made his customers feel at home. People came to expect it." She paused. "They still do."

Edward couldn't stop the smile that found its way to his lips. He found he often smiled when he looked at Maribeth. He looked forward to seeing her in the morning when she first arrived, usually a bit late and bedraggled, but still very pretty. Now, dressed in a yellow cotton dress with a white Peter Pan collar, she reminded him of a daisy. She exuded freshness and sunshine.

So why did he often think of her not wearing anything at all?

He cleared his throat and sat up straighter in his chair. "You know how these people are," he said, noting the hoarseness that had crept unsuspectingly into his voice. "They despise change."

"Edward—"

"Take the lobby, for instance. There's no telling how long it's been since the last paint job. Who would've thought people would complain when I changed it from cobweb-gray to apricot?"

"You're moving too fast for them, Edward. You come rolling into town in a fancy car and three-piece suits and expect to change everything overnight. Everything your grandfather stood for." She had to stop to catch her breath. She took in the clean-shaven face, then dropped her gaze to the column of throat that was ever-so-tan against the crisp white collar of his shirt. Some men looked restrained in business suits, but not Edward, Maribeth told herself. He wore his clothes as though they were part of him, a second skin, and although they awarded an air of formality to his appearance, they did not temper the blatant masculinity that lay beneath. But then, nothing could.

Edward returned her gaze. She was looking at him,

really looking at him, he thought. Male pride convinced him she wasn't oblivious to him after all. His eyes focused on her lips, their bow shape enhanced by a rich coral shade of lipstick. She licked them nervously and that delicate pink tongue was almost his undoing. His eyes zoomed in on her full bottom lip. He'd give up half his money market account to know what her relationship with that Moss fellow really was. "Tell me something," he said. "You don't agree with anything I'm doing here, do you?"

The question took her by surprise. "I'm only thinking of what's best for the bank. I'm not sure you have the bank's interests in mind when you make some of your decisions."

He chuckled. "Are you always so straightforward?"

"I try to be."

"You're not like most women I've known."

Maribeth bristled. "Is that your way of telling me I'm not sophisticated?"

He looked surprised. "Certainly not." He unfolded himself from the chair and walked slowly toward her, his eyes fastened to hers. He stopped only inches from her and gazed down at her in the chair, cocking his head to the side with an amused look. "My, your feathers get ruffled easily. You're a real Annie Oakley, aren't you?"

She stood out of anger, then wished she hadn't when she found herself only inches from him, looking directly into his face. "I don't like being compared to the sort of women you know."

He threw his head back and laughed. "And what sort would that be?"

"And I don't appreciate your making fun of me." She twirled around on her heels and started for the door. His hand closing around her wrist both surprised her and made it impossible to move.

"I was only trying to tell you I like your honesty, Maribeth," he said, all humor gone from his face. "You don't play games with people. I like that." He paused for a second. "And if I were to start comparing you to most of the women I've known, you'd come out on top every time."

She merely stared at him, not having the slightest idea how to respond. "I—I've always been honest," she finally said. "Honest to a fault, I guess you could say."

He gazed at her face, admiring the delicate line of her jaw, her unblemished peach complexion. "I like a woman who says what she thinks."

Maribeth realized he was still holding her wrist. His hand felt big and warm. She tugged her arm gently and he released her. She backed slowly out of his office, wanting to put some distance between them. His after-shave was making her giddy and just looking at him did strange things to her stomach. "Give me a few days," she said, trying to end their conversation on a casual note, "and we'll see if you still feel that way."

Moss Gentry was waiting for Maribeth when she got off work that afternoon. She came to an abrupt halt in the parking lot when she saw him leaning against her car. Moss. She had grown up with him, attended the same schools. They'd been best friends, buddies, conspirators. She smiled at the thought. They'd pulled so many pranks in high school, Maribeth couldn't help but wonder how they'd ever graduated.

Moss saw her and started walking toward her. Maribeth had forgotten how tall he was, six and a half feet with a barrel of a chest. If she hadn't already known he was a truck driver, she would have guessed him a lumberjack.

"Hello, Maribeth," he said. "You're looking good."

"Moss." She swallowed. "So are you," she said. "Thank you for the flowers," she added nervously.

He shrugged in answer. "Why don't we take a walk?" he suggested. "To the square."

She nodded and walked beside him. They talked about nonessential things on the way, being polite to each other as though they were strangers. Why couldn't it be like old times? Maribeth wondered. Why had Moss gone and spoiled it all with confessions of love? She could still remember the feeling of disbelief as he'd poured it out, long after graduation. She hadn't wanted to hurt him. She would never forget the pain in his eyes when she had told him she could never love him the way he wanted her to. He had refused to believe it.

When they finally reached the square, Maribeth took a seat on one of the benches. Moss sat beside her. "Why did you come back, Maribeth?" he asked flatly.

"Well," she began, not meeting his intense gaze. "I guess I found out I wasn't a big-city girl after all."

One corner of his mouth curled into a smile. "I think I remember telling you that myself, if memory serves me right."

She shrugged, watching the late-afternoon sun turn his hair bronze. "I suppose I had to learn it on my own."

"You had no business running off to Atlanta like that. Your place is here. With me."

"No, Moss," she said, shaking her head. After two years she would have thought he'd come to realize it himself.

"I still love you, Maribeth. I never stopped. I let you go to Atlanta because I always knew you'd come back. I worked my hump off to buy myself my own rig so I could afford to take on a wife and—"

"Stop it!" she said. "I told you two years ago how I felt, and nothing has changed. I'm not going to sit here and listen to this kind of talk. You'll only regret saying these things to me later." She stood up.

"Maribeth." The sound of his voice made her turn around. "You and I once meant a lot to each other. Don't throw that away."

"Then stop making it difficult to remain friends," she said, and walked away.

The next two weeks passed quickly for Maribeth, between unpacking and learning her new job, which she was determined to be nothing less than wonderful at. She and Edward had settled into something of a routine. Each morning they shared their first cup of coffee in Edward's office and discussed bank business.

"I'm going to install a drive-through window," he told Maribeth one morning, "and a twenty-four-hour computerized teller service."

Maribeth almost spilled her coffee. "Won't that be expensive?"

"We have to keep up with the times."

"You're moving too fast, Edward. I've already warned you." He only seemed to be half listening, she could tell he was already planning it to the last detail. "One of the customers complained yesterday about the old water cooler being replaced."

He looked surprised. "The thing only worked half the time," he said, "and you had to bang on it to get anything out of it."

"Precisely. But our customers got a kick out of it. Of course, they complained that the bank should put in a new one, but they didn't mean it."

Edward frowned. "Maribeth, you've totally confused me."

She sighed. "It's like the superette, Edward. Half the men in town hang out there. They sit around a potbellied stove on old crates and grumble that the owner should put in some chairs. Now, what do you think would happen if the owner *did* put in chairs?"

"I haven't the slightest idea."

"They'd say it wasn't the same anymore and probably find a new place to hang out." She saw the blank look on his face and wondered if he would ever come to understand the people in Laurel. "These people believe in tradition, Edward. And every time you make a change, it's like stripping away a part of their history, their memories." She paused and studied him for a moment. "Do you know what I think one of your problems is?"

He took a sip of his coffee. It tasted bitter, and he knew the old coffee urn needed to be replaced. But he wasn't about to mention it now after the uproar he'd caused replacing the water cooler. "No, but I have the distinct feeling you're going to tell me." In the past couple of weeks he'd learned just how honest she could be. Maribeth didn't mince words. She told it like it was.

"I think you're overdressed for this town."

"Overdressed?" He glanced down at his suit. "I happen to think I have fairly good taste in clothes."

She stood up. "You have excellent taste," she said, giving his dove-gray suit and melon shirt a thorough perusal. "But this isn't Wall Street, and people in this town only wear jackets to church on Sunday morning." She paused. "Have you ever stopped and noticed the way people dress here?"

"Yes, and I refuse to wear double-knit slacks and Ban-Lon shirts."

She glared at him. "You're hopeless."

"Okay, okay," he said, smiling at her show of temper. She was cute when she got angry, thrusting that delicate chin upward the way she did. "What are you suggesting?"

"That you merely dress less formal." She saw the doubtful look on his face. "You know how you're always complaining that nobody ever talks to you when you go into the superette for a cold drink?"

Edward frowned. The superette was a sore spot with him. He had given up his daily treks to the small grocery store across the street because he was always ignored by the other businessmen and women who dropped in from time to time for a cold drink and small talk.

"I'll make a bet with you," Maribeth said, moving closer to him. "Stand up and take off your jacket."

"Why? What are you going to do?"

"Trust me." She gave him an irresistible smile. "Not afraid I'll bite, are you?" She blushed at her own comment. What on earth had made her say that?

Edward unfolded himself from the chair slowly, like a cat, noting her discomfort with great amusement. "Go ahead," he said, a teasing lilt in his tone, "as long as you've had all your shots." He shrugged off his jacket and draped it across the back of the chair. "Okay, now what?"

"The vest," she said, and watched him remove it. The cotton shirt beneath was fitted and emphasized his wide shoulders and trim waist. His chest was broad. She swallowed and valiantly regained her composure. "Okay, now remove your tie." When he hesitated, she reached for it. "Let me," she offered, half afraid he wouldn't go along with her plan. She began loosening the tie, trying not to meet his eyes. When the loop was large enough, she slipped it over his head. It gave her a heady, exhilarating feeling doing something as bold as removing an article of his clothing, even if it was completely innocent. Next, while he was gazing down at her, thoroughly perplexed, she unbuttoned the cuffs on his shirt and rolled his sleeves to his elbows. He remained perfectly still, and she hoped he could not hear the heavy thudding of her heart. It was the first time she'd seen his bare arms and they were nice, she decided, slightly muscular and feathered with dark hair. Instinct told her the rest of his body would be equally hairy, and she blushed again in spite of herself.

Why couldn't she keep her mind off the poor man's body, for heaven's sake? She was obviously turning into some kind of sex maniac.

"Maribeth, would you mind telling me what this is all about?" he asked, chuckling. "I admit I like having you undress me, but I'm certain our thoughts aren't moving in the same direction."

"I want you to go over to the superette dressed like this and see if the people treat you any different."

"No. I've already told you I'm not setting foot back in that place."

"Then you'll have to drive to Wilson's Convenience across town to buy a soft drink," she said lightly. When that didn't seem to have any effect on him, she went on. "I'll even bet money on this."

Edward thought about it. The convenience store charged twice the price for everything and was more than a mile away. "Oh, all right," he muttered, "I'll go. Not because I think it's going to matter one way or the other, but because I know you won't stop nagging me until I do. When you get your mind on something, you just won't let go."

"I'm going with you."

He started out the door with her behind him. "Wait." He stopped abruptly. "Did you say this was a bet?"

She shrugged. "If you want it to be. I can only go as high as five dollars."

"No, I don't want your money; think of something else. If I win, that is to say, if I get snubbed by the people in the superette despite my clothes, what do I get?"

"What do you want?" The words had no sooner left her mouth than she realized her meaning could be misconstrued. Edward's wicked grin proved it. She blushed. "I think I should add, this is a good clean bet."

He looked only slightly crestfallen as he rubbed his chin in thought. "Let me see," he said, trying to think of something worthwhile. He snapped his fingers. "I've got it. If I win, you'll agree to be at work on time for one month."

Maribeth frowned. He was going for blood.

"And you'll have all your . . . uh, personal grooming completed by the time you walk through that front door." He grinned, knowing how tough it would be for her. She had to be one of the most unorganized people he'd ever met.

She gave him a cool look. "Are you finished?"

"Uh-huh."

"Then what do I get if I win?"

"You can have anything you want," he said in a voice that let her know he personally was up for grabs. She thought for a moment. "Okay, if I win, if someone in the superette is friendly to you, you'll agree to give me an extra fifteen minutes on my lunch hour."

His laugh was more of a snort. "You already do that anyway."

"And you'll stop complaining about my personal telephone calls."

"All of them except for that Moss fellow," he said. "Anything else?"

"I think that about does it," she said breezily, confident she would be the winner.

The sun was warm on her face as Maribeth crossed the street beside Edward. The superette stood directly across from the bank in a convenient location for everyone working or shopping in the small town. They both paused at the door before going in. "Ready?" she asked. Edward nodded. The heavy wooden door creaked loudly and a bell jingled at the top as he pushed it open.

Fifteen minutes later Maribeth and Edward walked out that same door, both of them holding a cold drink in their hand. "I don't believe it," Edward said, shaking his head in disbelief. "Hector Billings spoke to me."

Maribeth smiled, genuinely pleased with the results of her experiment. Hector Billings was the president of the Laurel Community Club, not to mention the veritable backbone of the town. Hector usually had the last say in anything that happened in Laurel. As they crossed the street Maribeth checked her wristwatch. "Well, I suppose I should go to lunch now."

Edward, who was beaming, dropped a glance at his own watch. "It's not twelve o'clock yet."

She stepped onto the curb that ran in front of the bank. "Yes, but now that I have a longer lunch break, I think I'll do some shopping." She hurried through the front door of the bank and made her way across the lobby with a frowning Edward following close behind. She walked into her office and grabbed her purse from a desk drawer. When she turned around, she almost bumped into him. "By the way"—she reached down for the pink message pad and handed it to him— "would you mind taking my calls while I'm out?" She started out the door.

"If Moss Gentry calls, I'm hanging up," he warned her, but she was already gone.

The following Friday Maribeth was finishing her work for the day when she glanced up and found Martha Hines, a widow who lived across town, standing in the doorway. Maribeth straightened and gave her a welcoming smile. "Come in, Martha," she invited. "Is there anything I can do for you?"

Martha walked through the door and handed Maribeth several envelopes. The woman looked as though she would burst into tears at the slightest provocation. "What's this?" Maribeth said. She looked inside one of the envelopes and found a pink slip of paper.

"Bank overdrafts," the woman said, her bottom lip quivering. "This bank is bouncing every check I write."

"Is there a problem?" a masculine voice asked, causing both Maribeth and Martha to jump.

Maribeth looked up and found Edward beside his door. "I'm afraid so. Mrs. Hines says we're . . . uh, bouncing all her checks."

Edward came closer. "I'm sorry if we've made a mistake, Mrs. Hines," he said politely. 'I'm sure it can be corrected immediately. When did you last make a deposit?"

"Several weeks ago. When my Social Security check came in."

Edward took the envelopes and glanced at the overdrafts inside. "What's your present balance?"

Martha's face reddened. "I—I'm not really sure. I've never been real good with figures. Melvin always handled that sort of thing."

"You don't know how much money you have in your checking account?" Edward asked, as though the mere thought was ludicrous.

"Edward, Mrs. Hines is a widow," Maribeth said, trying to quell the look of utter disbelief on his face. "Her husband has only been dead a couple of years and . . ." She let the sentence die, not knowing what else to say.

"Give me a few minutes and I'll check on this for you," he said, and hurried out of the office.

"Would you like a cup of end-of-the-day coffee, Martha?" Maribeth offered in an attempt to put the woman at ease.

"No, thank you." Martha took one of the chairs by the door and stared at her feet.

"Are you still making those adorable little Raggedy Ann and Andy dolls?" Maribeth asked, trying to start up a conversation.

Martha nodded and gave her a tight smile. "Yes, but they don't sell well this time of year. Folks usually order them around Christmas."

Edward was back a moment later. "Mrs. Hines, I'm afraid you have no money in your account. I checked and double-checked, but it comes up zero every time."

Martha Hines stood and sighed heavily. "I figured as much." She took the envelopes from Edward and stuffed them into her purse. Her bottom lip quivered so badly, she bit it. "I've never had a check bounce in my life, Mr. Spears," she said, trying to gather her composure. "I can't tell you how embarrassed I was to find these in my mailbox." Tears filled her eyes.

Maribeth, feeling as though she might cry as well, reached for the box of tissue on her desk and handed it to Martha, who began mopping her tears.

"I'm a widow, Mr. Spears, and I'm having a hard time making ends meet on my Social Security check," Martha continued, not looking into Edward's eyes. "I take in sewing and do a little cleaning here and there, but it's still hard." This time she met his gaze. "Your grandfather knew how hard I had it. He never bounced my checks. When I got behind, he would call me up and ask me if he could help out, and I would scrape together what I could to cover my checks. But he never sent me no pink slips."

"Mrs. Hines," Edward said gently, "I can certainly understand your situation, but do you have any idea what would happen to this bank if we suddenly stopped sending pink slips and let our customers write bad checks to their hearts' delight?"

Martha Hines didn't seem to be listening. "Your grandfather was a good man, Mr. Spears. He cared about his customers. I plan to make these checks good as soon as my next Social Security check comes in." One fat tear rolled down her cheek. "Then as soon as we're even, I'd like to come in and close out my account."

"Mrs. Hines, that isn't necessary," he said.

"Maybe not for you, but it is for me. After this, I'd be embarrassed to death to set foot in this bank." She gave Maribeth a watery smile and left the room.

Maribeth rounded her desk and sank into her chair, holding her head in both hands. All she could think of was the look on Martha Hines's face.

"What's wrong with you?" Edward asked.

"That should be obvious," she muttered.

"The Hines woman?" He didn't wait for her to answer. "Look, Maribeth, I feel sorry for the woman too, okay? I'd hate for my mother to be in that predicament, but that doesn't mean she should be allowed to write checks that she can't possibly cover."

"Even if it means going without food, Edward?" she asked, looking up at him. "When the refrigerator is empty, and her next check is a week away, what is the poor woman supposed to do?"

"Okay." He raised both hands as if to surrender. "We'll toss out the pink slips and let our customers write all the bad checks they like."

"Now you're being ridiculous."

"Of course, that means we'll soon be out of a job because the bank won't have any money, but that's all right because at least we didn't let anybody go hungry." He paused. "This isn't the Salvation Army, Maribeth."

She stood up, her eyes flashing with anger. "You know what your problem is?"

"Here we go again."

"Your idea of banking is making sure all the figures and ledgers add up. You couldn't care less about the people you deal with, your customers. Banking has nothing to do with figures and computer printouts, Edward. It has to do with people. Your grandfather knew that. That's why he was so successful. You'll never be the man he was. Never! Because you don't give a damn about people!" She had to stop to catch her breath. "Now, go ahead and fire me."

Instead of firing her, Edward walked into his office. How long they each sat at their desks in silence, Maribeth didn't know, but she finally got up and walked to the doorway of his office. He was sitting in his chair staring off into space. Scattered across his desk were various brochures and seed catalogs. "What's that for?" she asked, motioning toward them.

He glanced down at the pile as though he had forgotten about them. He leaned forward and began stacking them neatly. "I figured I should do some reading on fertilizers," he said. "The subject comes up frequently at the superette, and I thought it wouldn't hurt to know something about it, just in case someone wanted my opinion." He smiled bitterly. "But we both know that's not likely to happen, don't we?"

"Edward—" She paused, not knowing what to say. Instead, she sank into one of the chairs in front of his desk.

"Also I had thought about growing my own garden one day." He leaned back in his chair and planted his hands behind his head. "Is that the most ridiculous thing you've ever heard or what?"

"Are you feeling sorry for yourself?"

"Maybe." He glanced at her. "Are we going to fight again?"

She folded her hands in her lap and stared at them. "I had no right to spout off like that. You're the president of the bank; you're the one who has to make the decisions, not me."

Edward wasn't listening. His eyes were focused on the picture of his grandfather that hung above one of the file cabinets. He studied it, taking in the strong jaw and dominant nose that made their resemblance so strong. Why hadn't he gotten to know him better? He sighed. "James Edward Spears, the First," he said out loud. "You're a tough act to follow, old man."

Maribeth knew he was hurting. "So are you," she said, feeling the need to defend him, even to himself.

He dropped his gaze from the picture and settled it on her. "I think that's the nicest thing anyone has said to me in a long time." His gaze lingered on her face, then dipped briefly to her soft breasts before climbing back up to her hair, which was tied back primly with a scarf. He chuckled. "You know, you're the only friend I have in this town, and sometimes I even wonder about that."

"Oh? I would have thought you would have a few lady friends by now."

He grinned as he hauled himself up from the chair and made his way slowly around the desk. He deposited himself on the edge of his desk directly in front of her. "Would it bother you?" he asked hopefully. It had never occurred to him that it might.

Maribeth refused to meet his eyes. Instead, she kept looking intently at the front of his shirt. He'd settled nicely into his new work attire, having dispensed with the coat and tie, and although he was still the epitome of neatness, his new look was disarmingly sexy. "Let's just say I wouldn't be surprised."

He threw his head back and laughed, a full rich sound that sent tingles across Maribeth's flesh. "I somehow knew you would find a way to avoid the question." He reached down and took both of her hands in his, then pulled her up so that she was standing in front of him, caught between his hard thighs. She held her breath as he untied the scarf at her neck and pulled her hair free. Maribeth could only stand there, held fast by his intensity.

She was not prepared for the kiss, even as his face lowered to hers.

Edward's lips claimed hers as though they had every right to do so. Maribeth was too shocked to do anything about it. His mouth was warm as it moved over hers in a kiss that could only be described as devastating. Big hands snaked around her waist and pulled her close, pressing her intimately against the V of his thighs. His after-shave permeated her senses and turned her knees to putty. She had no other choice but to cling to him. His lips coaxed a response, and she answered it eagerly, parting her lips so he could explore the depths beyond. When he raised his head, he was smiling. Instinctively she pulled back, but he refused to let her go. She was trembling from head to toe. How could one kiss be so potent? Maribeth asked herself.

"I can honestly say that this is more fun than fighting with you," he said. When he saw the look of outright shock on her face, he shrugged. "I only meant to kiss you as a friend," he confessed, surprised by his own ardent display. Her full bottom lip was quivering, still moist from his kiss. He wanted to take that lip between his teeth and— He sighed heavily at the familiar ache in his loins and hoped he wouldn't give himself away. "I guess I got carried away, huh?" he said, giving her a sheepish smile.

Maribeth was stunned. Carried away? *Carried away?* Was that all he could say when, for her, the earth had moved? Well, she could be just as cool as the next person if she had to. No doubt he was used to more sophisticated women. She probably had *hick* written all over her face. "Oh, that's okay," she said, trying to sound casual, determined not to let him see how it had affected her. "Think nothing of it." She waved the matter off as though it had about as much signifigance as the contents of her wastebasket. She didn't see his frown, as she glanced at her wristwatch. "Oh, my, it's well after five. I've got to go." The truth was she had to get out of there before her knees buckled. She hurried out of his office.

He followed her. He could still taste her on his lips. It left him wanting more. "Big weekend planned?" he asked, the frown still lurking in his eyes. He wasn't sure he wanted to know how and with whom she spent her weekends. Would Moss Gentry be on her list? He knew very little about the man other than what he could dig up at the superette without being obvious. He watched her pull her pocketbook out of her bottom desk drawer. When she straightened, she was smiling at him as though nothing had happened. It irritated him. True, his kisses had never sent women swooning to the hospital, but he'd at least gotten some kind of reaction.

"I don't really have big plans for the weekend," she said, a bit too breezily. She cleared off the rest of her desk. "I'm just meeting friends, some of the tellers actually, at Jake's Tavern for a beer."

"Mind if I join you?" It was out before he knew it.

She looked up in surprise. "Why would you want to do that?" she blurted out without thinking. "I mean, it's not very fancy."

"I wouldn't have asked if I didn't want to go."

"Well—" How was she going to keep up this cool facade when every time she looked at him she thought of that kiss?

"We could take my car."

My, but he was persistent. "Uh, I guess so."

He rewarded her with a smile. "Just let me get my jacket." He turned for his office, but stopped abruptly at the door and laughed. "I keep forgetting I don't wear a jacket anymore." He followed her out into the hall. "Are you sure you don't mind being seen with me?" he asked, dropping the smile. "I'm not the most popular man in town, you know."

"I can't think of anyone I'd rather be seen with," she said, and the look of surprise on his face was nothing compared to her own.

Three

"This Jake fellow must do one heck of a business," Edward said, guiding his older-model Mercedes around the concrete building for the second time.

"Friday nights are his busiest," Maribeth said. She pointed quickly to a space where a car had just pulled out. She wanted out of the car. Sitting in the next office from Edward was a whole lot different from sharing the close confines of his car. And, of course, she hadn't stopped thinking about the kiss. She was out of the car before he cut the engine.

Edward held the door open for her so she could pass first into the dimly lit tavern. She blinked her eyes against the gloom until she spotted the other employees, grouped together at a round table in the back. She waved and headed in their direction with Edward close behind. Sitting at the table were a couple of tellers; Ted Jones, who handled mortgage loans; and Carol McCloy and her husband, Dan. Maribeth took the empty chair next to Dan's while Edward went in search of an extra. When he returned, he planted it next to hers. He shook Dan's hand as soon as they were introduced, then greeted the other people at the table.

"So how's the carpet business, Dan?" Maribeth asked, smiling at him fondly. She'd always liked Dan. A hard worker, he'd come from a poor family, but hadn't let that stop him from making a success of himself.

"I can't complain," he said, returning the smile.

Maribeth was prevented from saying anything further as Jake Brownlee, the tavern owner, came up beside her. As usual, he had a mouthful of chewing gum. "What'll you have, Maribeth?" he asked gruffly. Jake looked like a mountain standing over her. He sometimes frightened off strangers with his enormous size and surly disposition. His face was half hidden beneath a snarled black beard and bushy brows that had a tendency to frown. He looked more pirate than tavern owner.

"Just give me a draft," she said, sending him a winning smile.

"I'll have a Heineken," Edward said, when Jake looked at him.

Jake blew a bubble and popped it. "I don't carry imported beer. Just plain ol' draft. If you want something fancy you'll have to go to the next town."

"I'll have a draft," Edward said dutifully.

"Good choice, Slick," Dan McCloy said, giving Edward a friendly wink. "Make that three drafts, Jake," he added. He waited until Jake left the table before he said anything more. "Don't mind Jake," he told Edward. "I know he looks like a grizzly bear and doesn't act that friendly, but he would give you the shirt off his back if you needed it."

"Yeah, but who could possibly fill out a shirt that size?" Edward asked wryly. Dan threw his head back and laughed.

One of the tellers stood up. "I'd better get home," she said, smiling wanly at the group. "My kids will wonder where I've been."

"Me too," another girl said, standing as well. Ted

Jones joined them. "Actually we all rode together," he said sheepishly to explain why they were all leaving so quickly and at the same time. Maribeth bristled in silence, wondering if their departure had anything to do with Edward's surprise appearance.

Dan shrugged. "Carol and I can stay."

"For a while," Carol said, "but we have to be at Mother's by six-thirty, remember?"

Dan winced. "Yeah, I *did* forget. We're having dinner there tonight." He looked at Edward. "I'd better not be late for that. It's the only time I get a decent meal." Carol slapped him playfully on the arm, and he pretended to be injured.

Jake brought their drinks, and the group was silent as he passed them out. When he left, Dan was the first to speak. "So you're the fancy New York banker I've been hearing about. Carol says you're the greatest boss in the world." He grinned when his wife blushed. "What in the world made you decide to move to this hick town, Slick?" he asked, cocking his head to the side.

Edward laughed good-naturedly. "My grandfather left me most of his holdings when he died. I was fed up with big-city life so I figured I'd give this a try. And"—he paused briefly—"I wanted to find out why my grandfather loved this town so much."

"Old man Spears was a good man," Dan said, nodding thoughtfully.

"I wish I had known him better."

"Well, Carol and I certainly wish you the best, Slick," Dan said, toasting Edward with his beer.

They talked among themselves a few more minutes until Dan finished his beer. "We'd best be on our way," he said, looking at his wife. "Don't want to make Mother angry." He reached over and shook Edward's hand. "Let's do this again sometime."

"I'd like that." Edward stood as Carol rose from the

table. The couple said their good-byes and walked out of the tavern arm in arm.

Edward took his chair and turned to Maribeth. "Well? Don't you have some place you need to be?"

She shrugged. "I suppose I should go home and feed my cats."

"Can I buy you another beer before we go?"

"I'll split one with you," she said, eager to have an excuse to stay for a while longer. "Besides, we came in your car, remember?"

"Oh, right." He motioned for Jake to bring them another beer. The man nodded sharply, and Edward wondered if he would or not. "I appreciate you inviting me here with your friends," he said to Maribeth.

"I didn't invite you. You invited yourself."

He grinned. "That's right, I did, didn't I?" His gaze dropped from hers to her lips and he remembered distinctly what she tasted like. "You seem to know a lot of people here."

"I should. I've lived here all my life." She noticed his eyes kept darting to her lips, and it made her uneasy. "I lost touch with most of my close friends when I moved to Atlanta."

Edward nodded as Jake set the beer down in front of him. "Why did you move to Atlanta in the first place?" he asked her once they were alone again.

She shrugged. "I thought I was missing out on something by being cooped up in this small town. So when Peg, my best friend, suggested it, I was all for it." She paused. "I suppose I had other reasons," she added, as though talking to herself.

"Did Moss Gentry have anything to do with it?" he asked, knowing he was getting personal. He couldn't help it. He had to know.

"Maybe."

He poured some of his beer into her glass. Her coral lipstick had smudged the glass where her lips had been, and he couldn't help but think how nice it would be to have coral smudges all over his body. His hand shook as he handed her the glass. "Is that your way of saying it's none of my business?" he asked, giving her a funny half smile.

Maribeth sighed and took a sip of her beer. "Moss and I go way back," she said. "As far back as I can remember. We climbed trees together, fished together." She laughed. "I can't begin to tell you some of the skirmishes the two of us got into." She stopped talking and looked at him. "Are you sure you want to hear this?"

"I'm listening."

"After graduation Moss attended some truck driver's school in Columbia, and I went to the community college in the next town. Moss came home weekends, and we spent all our time together like we always had." She paused. "I'm not sure when I first noticed a change in him. I think it was after he had started working for a trucking firm. He'd come home on weekends, and I'd casually mention going someplace with one of the guys we both knew and Moss would start questioning me about it. I just thought he was being protective. Like a big brother. Know what I mean?" She saw Edward nod and continued. "The fact is, Moss was jealous. He was in love with me." She shook her head as though she still found it hard to believe.

Edward watched her expressive eyes as she talked. They were hazel. For weeks he had wondered about the color, unable to decide if they were blue or green, and had finally simply asked her. "How did you find out?"

"He just up and told me one day. Said he'd loved me for years. I never even suspected. I mean, he'd never so much as tried to kiss me. How was I supposed to know?"

"What did you do?"

She ran her finger around the rim of her glass absently. "At first I was so shocked, I didn't know what to say. But I had to tell him the truth. I mean, I love Moss dearly, always have, but—"

"But not the way he wanted you to, right?" Edward said, feeling slightly guilty over his relief.

She nodded. "But Moss wouldn't take no for an answer. He's kind of a bully, used to having his own way. Anyway, it all happened about the same time Peg started talking about moving to Atlanta. I was twenty-one with a good enough education to make it on my own, so I went." She shook her head and gave Edward a wry smile. "I can't begin to tell you the scene Moss and I had. You see, I always did pretty much what Moss wanted. He was the leader and I followed. But by moving to Atlanta, I defied him. I think that's what hurt him most."

"And now?"

"He insists his feelings haven't changed."

"How do you feel?" Edward was uncomfortable discussing another man with Maribeth, but he was determined to get some answers to the questions he'd been asking himself over and over lately.

"Like a heel," she answered.

"Maribeth, you can't force yourself to love someone."

"I know." She laughed self-consciously. "I can't believe I'm telling you all this. Let's change the subject."

"All right." He was tired of hearing about Moss Gentry anyway. "Did you like living in Atlanta?"

"At first. But I was homesick a lot. Peg loved it. That's one of the reasons I stayed as long as I did. Then, when she got married, I decided it was time to come home."

Edward noticed the sadness lurking in her eyes. Was it Moss or just her memories? The Maribeth he'd come to know was strong and capable. Could it be she was soft and vulnerable as well? That thought made him want to look deeper inside of her. "Are you glad to be back?" he asked.

She'd been studying his fingers on his glass and looked up in surprise. "It's where I belong." She leaned back in her chair, tired of talking about herself. "What about you? Are you happy here? Weren't you happy in New York?"

"Happy enough," he said. "But I was getting tired of traffic jams and waiting in lines and all the noise." He settled back in his chair as well. "I spent two weeks here the summer I turned ten. It was the happiest time of my life. I had planned to come back, of course, but the following summer I was involved with swim lessons and baseball. The older I got, the more I had going on in my life." His expression became forlorn. "My grandmother died during finals in college. I flew down for the funeral but couldn't stay. After college I went right to work." He frowned into his glass. "Then my grandfather died, and it was too late."

"It's not too late," she said. "You're here now, aren't you?" She laid her hand on his, feeling the sudden need to reach out to him. His eyes met hers for a moment, and she felt her stomach flutter from the intensity of his gaze. She pulled her hand away.

"Yes, I'm here now, but for how long?"

Her eyebrows bunched together at the top of her nose. "What's that supposed to mean?"

He leaned both elbows on the table. "I was hoping business would have picked up by now," he answered, "and people would have accepted me. But they keep comparing me to my grandfather, and I always come out on bottom."

"It's going to take time, Edward."

"I've already been here a couple of months," he reminded her. "They're no closer to accepting me now than they were then."

"What are you going to do?"

"I'm not sure." He looked into his glass once again as though it might offer some answers. "I've never been a quitter, Maribeth, but at the same time, I've always made practical business decisions. It's not practical for me to keep losing money with the bank." He gave her a weak smile. "We both know there are a lot of people doing their banking in the next town. That's why I have so much time to study seed catalogs and do cross-word puzzles."

"I don't want to see you close the bank, Edward," she said, even though she understood his point. "Do you realize how much that bank means to this town, how long it has been a major part of this town?" She didn't wait for him to answer. "Why, my grandparents opened their first bank account with your grandfather forty years ago."

"I understand what you're saying, Maribeth," he said gently, "but you can't expect me to keep the bank running at a loss. If people can't accept me as a member of this community, they're certainly not going to trust me with their hard-earned money."

"You're absolutely right," she said, pondering his words.

Both brows arched up in surprise. "I am?" He chuckled. "Well, that's a first. You don't usually agree with me so easily."

Maribeth wasn't really listening. "You can't give up yet, Edward," she said. "I think I know a way to get these people to accept you." She leaned forward and whispered conspiratorially, "I have a plan."

"Oh-oh. The last time you had a plan, somebody got shot."

"I did *not* shoot Barney," she reminded for the umpteenth time. "I merely grazed his hand. Which, I might add, is healing wonderfully."

"How do you know?"

She gave him a beguiling smile. "I visit those two

men every Saturday at the county jail just to make sure Sheriff Hanks is treating them okay. And their real names are Figaro and Walter."

Edward shook his head. The woman was an enigma. "Okay, Gunsmoke, what's the plan?"

"First, tell me this. Do you trust me?"

He considered it for a moment. "I suppose so. You probably saved my life."

"My plan won't work unless you promise to do exactly as I say. Agreed?"

"Wait a minute. You haven't even told me what your plan is. I'm not going to agree to something I know nothing about."

She shrugged. "Then forget I said anything." She sipped her beer.

He crossed his arms and studied her. What did he have to lose? For some strange reason all her harebrained ideas seemed to work. "Okay," he said, wondering what he was getting himself into. "I'll agree to it if it's going to help me save the bank. What's the plan?"

She gave him a smug look. "Simple. I'm going to make you the most popular man in Laurel."

Edward rubbed his jaw as he gazed at her, trying to determine whether she was serious. She darn sure looked serious. "Just how do you hope to accomplish that?"

"I'm going to teach you how to look and act like the people in this town."

"Why?"

"So they'll accept you as one of them, why else?"

"I kind of like myself the way I am," he said defensively.

"Of course, you do. All I'm asking you to do is try things their way for a while. Dress like them, learn what they like to eat, socialize with them a bit. Maybe it will help you understand them better."

"Socialize with them? I haven't exactly been overwhelmed with invitations," he said dryly.

"That's because people are afraid you won't appreciate their simple functions after having lived in New York City." She paused. "In the future you won't need an invitation. You can go as my guest." Her eyes crept slowly to his for a reaction. His unwavering gaze made her uneasy. She rubbed her hands together and found her palms damp. "What do you say?"

"What about Moss Gentry?"

She looked away. "You let me worry about Moss."

"Yeah, but is he going to beat my brains out when he sees us together?"

"I'll personally claw his eyes out if he lays a hand on you."

"You mean, after I'm dead?"

"We don't have to do this, you know."

"Forget what I said," Edward told her, giving her a smug look. "I happen to know a little jujitsu. I can take care of myself."

"What the heck is that?"

"It's a form of judo. I'm quite good at it actually. So if Moss Gentry decides to come after me, it'll be his head on a platter, not mine." He hoped he sounded more confident than he felt. He'd only seen Moss once, as he and Maribeth had walked to the square one day, and Moss was even bigger than Jake Brownlee. He probably ate tree trunks for breakfast, Edward thought. "Just one more question, Maribeth. Why are you doing this?"

His question startled her. She'd been gazing at his shirt collar which was unbuttoned and formed a V at his neck. She knew if she pressed her lips against the pulse at his throat she would be rewarded with textures and fragrances like no other. She already knew what the inside of his mouth tasted like. "I'm doing it because I need my job," she said, blinking furiously to unclog her brain, which had just refused to function. She returned her gaze to his. "What do you think will happen to your employees if you close the bank?"

"I've thought of that," he said. "I would make the necessary provisions."

"I can't hope for much severance pay after three weeks work."

"So you're doing it for job security."

"And friendship."

"Friendship?" He looked amused. "Is that what you call this thing between us, Maribeth?"

She almost shivered at the husky sound of his voice but avoided the question like one would avoid plunging into ice water. "I think this town needs that bank," she said flatly. She saw the disappointment in his eyes and knew he'd wanted an answer to his question. But how could she answer when she had no idea herself what her feelings were? She needed time.

Edward knew his question had made her uneasy, but he would have given anything for an answer, anything to go on. She'd been hedging all evening. Why? "What if your plan doesn't work?" he asked, getting back to the subject at hand. The last thing he wanted to do was scare her off.

"If it doesn't work, you can close the bank down with a clear conscience, knowing you gave it your best shot. But before you can make a success with the bank, I think you need to understand the people that you're serving. You need to learn their names, their children's names, their grandchildren's names. Your grandfather knew all this."

"Yes, but he had forty years to learn it."

"You aren't going to have that much time," she said simply. Her smile was encouraging. "Don't worry. You'll catch on."

He considered it all. "Okay," he finally said. "When do we start?"

She glanced at her watch and saw it was still early. "Tonight if you like. First we have to get you out of those clothes."

"Mmm. I can tell I'm going to like this already," he said, giving her a wicked grin. "Do you get to take off yours as well?"

"Very funny," she said, although her stomach dipped slightly at the thought. "Well, let's get started." She shoved her chair away from the table. "Before you change your mind."

"This is not exactly what I had in mind when you said you wanted to get me out of my clothes," Edward said, standing in front of a three-way mirror in the men's department of a local retail store. "What do you think? Do I look like a good ol' boy from South Carolina?"

Maribeth tried not to stare at his backside, but darn, the man looked good in blue jeans! The denim material stretched nicely across his slender hips and molded to his thighs in a way that made her mouth go dry. The cotton shirt fit him to a T and emphasized shoulders she was certain could support a porch swing. The top two buttons of his shirt were undone and a few sprigs of dark hair curled at the collar.

"You'll do," she said breathlessly, trying to make her voice sound natural. "Why don't you pick out a couple of shirts?" She held up several from which to choose. "If we hurry, we can make it to Lou's Shoes before they close."

"Why do we need to go there?" Edward asked, trying to select a shirt that wouldn't make him look as though he'd just joined the rodeo circuit. They were all designed with a western flair, in colors that were a bit bold for his taste. He finally decided, what the heck, and selected two of the gaudiest.

"You need to buy a pair of boots," she answered.

He frowned instantly. "Oh, no, I don't," he said, going back into the men's dressing room. He continued to talk from the other side of the door. "I don't like boots and I never have. I'm a banker, Maribeth, not a cowpoke."

"Which boot would you like to try, sir?" the saleslady at Lou's Shoes asked.

Edward glared at Maribeth. "Surely you don't expect me to wear cowboy boots with a four-hundred-dollar suit?"

"You don't wear suits anymore, remember?" She held up a pair of black boots trimmed in burgundy. "What do you think of these?"

"I hate them."

"He'll try these on," she told the saleslady.

"What size do you need, sir?" the woman asked.

He sighed heavily, the corners of his mouth turned downward in a frown. "Ten and a half."

Several minutes later Edward slipped on the boots. "I wouldn't be caught dead in these things."

"In that case I'll make sure you're not buried in them," Maribeth said. She smiled at the saleslady. "We'll take them."

"That will be ninety-five dollars and sixty cents," the woman said.

"You expect me to pay almost one hundred dollars for something I hate?" Edward asked Maribeth.

She smiled sweetly at the salesclerk. "May we please have a moment to discuss this?" The woman nodded and moved away. Maribeth crossed her arms and took a deep breath. "Look, Edward," she began in a voice of warning, "if you're going to complain about everything I suggest, then you can forget our little plan. You agreed to go along with everything I said."

"You didn't tell me I was going to have to dress like the Lone Ranger," he muttered. "I'll look like an idiot."

"That's the most ridiculous thing I've ever heard. Half the men in town would love to own those boots."

"Great. Let the store auction them off to the highest bidder."

"Okay," she said, throwing her hands in the air. "The deal's off."

He frowned. "How can you back out on a deal after only an hour?"

"Because you're not keeping up with your end of it, which is trying to dress like the people in this town. You obviously don't care if you have to close the bank."

"I didn't say that. That's the last thing I want."

"Then buy the boots," she pleaded in exasperation, "and let's get out of here. They're ready to close." She was beginning to think she'd made a mistake by offering to help. They were already fighting.

He planted both hands on his hips. "You're one heck of a bossy lady, you know that?" He cocked his head to one side and gazed down at her for a moment. His smile was almost brazen. "I think I may like taking you down a couple of notches."

The lump in her throat had nothing to do with his threat, she realized, as her eyes took in his impudent stance. He epitomized cocky male self-confidence. Her eyes wandered from his broad chest to his waist, to the expensive leather belt he wore, then dropped briefly to his thighs before returning slowly to his face. His threat was idle, she knew, but not the sensual message. He didn't have to throw his weight around the way Moss did to prove he was a man. He was subtle. Yet maleness seemed to exude from every pore of his body. Their eyes met and locked briefly, and his message was clear. He wanted her. All she had to do was say when.

"I'm just trying to help you, Edward," she finally said, trying desperately to regain her composure.

He sighed. "Okay, I'll buy the boots. But I refuse to wear them to work. Is that clear?"

"You're the boss."

"Oh, yeah? Then why do I feel I'm always on the

losing end?" He didn't wait for her to answer. He sat down and tried to pull one of the boots off. It wasn't as easy as it looked; the boot wouldn't budge.

"Let me help you," Maribeth offered. "Heaven knows, I've done this enough times for my father to do it with my eyes closed." She stepped between Edward's legs, bent over, and grabbed one booted foot, unaware her shapely behind was right in his face. "Okay, ready?" she asked, taking a firm grip on the boot.

His anger vanished. "Uh, what am I supposed to do?"

"Just hang on to the chair," she said, taking a deep breath. She pulled the boot with all her might. Edward gripped the chair tightly, not to keep from sliding off it but to keep his hands from reaching out and stroking her tempting fanny. Her hips were slender but plump enough to be curvaceous and very feminine. And sexy as all get-out. The boot popped off. "Okay, other foot," she announced in a tone that assured Edward she wasn't getting as much out of the experience as he was.

"Ready to go?" she asked, once he'd slipped on his dress shoes. "We need to pick up my car, then stop by my apartment."

Edward was still having trouble concentrating. "Why?"

She smiled at him as they walked toward the cash register, grateful he'd taken her advice on the boots, despite the fact he hated them. It proved he trusted her. "I have to feed my cats, and you need to change clothes." At his blank look she went on. "I'm taking you out on the town tonight."

After stopping by the bank so Maribeth could pick up her car, Edward followed her to her building, a gargantuan nineteenth-century house that had been renovated and divided into small apartments. It still retained its old-fashioned charm with its wraparound porch lined with rockers. "I like this," he said as he climbed out of his car. He followed her up an outside staircase that led to her apartment, his sacks and packages tucked under one arm. Camellia bushes near the stairs sweetened the air.

Maribeth slipped her key into the lock. "Get ready," she warned. "You're about to be attacked by two hungry cats." She pushed the door open and felt for the light switch. She flipped it on, revealing a clean but cluttered kitchen. Two plump cats scurried across the room to greet her.

"They don't look as though they've ever missed a meal," he said, dumping his packages on the counter.

"Meet Raisin Bran and Corn Flake," she introduced, stroking each cat affectionately.

"You named your cats after cereal brands?"

She shrugged. "It seemed a good idea at the time. Do you have any pets?"

"Once, for a short time. But I have a preference for dogs, and it's not easy to keep a dog in the city."

"Oh, I forgot. You're from New York."

He chuckled. "Try not to make it sound like a disease. Now, would you mind pointing me to the bathroom? I need to change into my new clothes so I can run out and start roping bulls or something."

Edward shook his head at his reflection in the mirror. He chuckled softly as he picked up the clothes he'd changed from and folded them neatly. He spotted the bottle of perfume on the counter and couldn't resist putting it to his nose. Yes, that was the scent. WILD HONEYSUCKLE the label read. Nice. Very nice. Did Maribeth realize what it did to him? Did she realize how attracted he was to her? Of course, that was the main reason he was going along with her plan—to spend more time with her. In the meantime he wasn't going to let her down. He could learn how to get along with a rattlesnake if he had to.

Maribeth gasped aloud when she saw him. John Travolta stand back, she thought, letting her gaze wander over Edward's jean-clad body. The banker had completely disappeared. He looked like someone who'd just hired on at a dude ranch, lean and rugged and devastatingly handsome. "My, don't you look nice," she said. Nice? She frowned at her choice of words. *Nice* wasn't the word for it. Those thighs encased in denim were more than tempting. She turned away to keep from staring.

"I hope you mean that," he said, watching her water one of the many plants she owned. "I feel like an idiot." He glanced at the living room, taking in the overstuffed couch and chair in a pretty country print. He liked her apartment. It was neat enough but had that cluttered, lived-in look. He wouldn't feel bad about littering her couch with the Sunday newspaper. As much as he liked her apartment, though, he found his eyes riveted to her snug-fitting jeans. She had changed from her dress, and although he hated giving up the sight of those long slender legs, he was content to stare at her cute behind. She leaned over to examine a brown-tipped leaf, and her derriere struck the same tempting pose it had in the store. His thoughts ran amok. He sucked in his breath sharply and turned for the kitchen. "Mind if I get myself a drink of water?" he asked, his speech unnaturally stilted.

"Help yourself. There's a three-month-old bottle of wine under the sink." She joined him a few minutes later, and found him leaning against a cabinet holding a glass of water. "I'm ready when you are," she said, noticing the tense lines in his face. "Are you okay?" When he nodded, she smiled. "I thought we might have dinner at the J&M Restaurant tonight. They're serving all the fried chicken you can eat for three ninety-five."

"Do they serve anything other than chicken?"

"Don't you like chicken?" She couldn't imagine someone not liking fried chicken. Why, that was almost un-American.

He gave her a grim look. "I worked in a place called King Chicken for two years during college. That just about did it for me where chicken is concerned."

"Don't tell me you worked to put yourself through college," she said. "I kind of got the idea your parents were well-to-do."

"Oh, they do all right," he said. "But my father has this tough-as-nails attitude about money. He paid my tuition and room and board, but it was up to me to work for the money for everything else. He figured it would teach me how to manage money on my own."

"Did it?"

He smiled. "Yeah. If I blew my week's check on partying, I ate chicken until my next payday. I got to where I dreamed about chicken."

"So what do you usually eat?"

"Steak or hamburger. Or frozen pizza. This town doesn't have a pizza parlor."

"You'll have to drive to the next town for that. I had no idea you hated chicken."

"I don't hate it," he said, correcting her, "I'm just not overly fond of it."

"Then you'd best not accept any dinner invitations in this town, 'cause that's all they cook around here."

"And if I'm invited someplace where they're serving it, I'll eat every last morsel. Now, are we going to fight about this or may we leave?"

Maribeth shot him a look of pure exasperation as she grabbed her purse. "I thought after dinner we could see a movie," she said, once they were outside. "I'd like to show you what this town has to offer in the way of entertainment as well as expose you to the townspeople."

He stopped at the top of the stairs. "Expose me?"

She laughed. "You know what I mean. I want to introduce you to as many people as I can."

He followed her down the stairs. "It makes sense. What's playing at the movies?"

"It's a double feature. *Nightmare on Elm Street* and *The Mummy.*"

"You're pulling my leg, right?"

She came to a halt at the bottom of the steps. "No I'm not. Don't you like horror films?"

Edward hesitated. After confessing his dislike for chicken, he wasn't about to tell her he hated horror movies. "I'm crazy about them," he said. "And you say it's double-feature night? Imagine that!" Maribeth rewarded him with a smile so dazzling, he was glad he'd lied.

"I had no idea you liked them," she said, walking beside him to his car. "I sometimes sit up half the night watching *Shock Theatre* on television."

When they reached his car, he opened the door for her. "That won't be necessary, Edward," she said. "Since this isn't a real date, I don't expect you to bother with the formalities."

"It's really no bother," he said, trying to sound cool and businesslike. "I like to keep in practice just in case the real thing comes along."

That thought was not at all pleasing to her.

The parking lot was crowded at the J&M. Half the town usually showed up on Friday night, and Jack and Marge, the owners, often had to call in the whole family to work.

"Now, don't be nervous," Maribeth said as they walked from the parking lot to the front door. "Act casual."

They entered the noisy restaurant side by side. Maribeth waved to several people she recognized as she scanned the room for an empty table. Jack and Marge's oldest son escorted them to a booth in the back that was being cleaned. As they made their way toward it,

Maribeth paused briefly beside a few tables to introduce Edward. She figured the more people saw of him, the better his chances would be of gaining acceptance into the small but tightly knit community.

Edward was aware of the looks he was receiving. "These people are staring at my boots," he muttered, as he took a seat across from her in the booth.

Maribeth's lips were pursed in annoyance. "If you're speaking of that table of teenage girls, it's not your boots they're staring at, it's your behind."

"Oh?" He glanced at the table of girls, and one waved. When he turned his attention back to Maribeth, he was grinning. "I suppose a man has to live with some things, huh?"

She glared at him. "When I said I wanted to get you out in front of people, I didn't mean you had to strut your stuff."

He leaned forward. "Did you say strut?" His eyes were amused. "I'm not strutting, Maribeth. If I seem to be walking funny that's only because these boots hurt my feet."

Maribeth buried her face in a menu. Why should she care if a group of immature girls flirted with Edward? She certainly didn't have any claim on him. Just because her heart slammed to her throat every time he looked at her and her knees threatened to buckle whenever he touched her, didn't mean the feeling was mutual. Besides, all they did was argue.

"I haven't seen one of these in a long time," Edward said, pointing to an antique jukebox selector on the wall. "What would you like to hear?"

"Play J-Seven," she mumbled, thankful for the diversion.

He looked up the number on the vinyl-coated pages. "Who is Merle Haggard?"

"He's a country-western singer. He has a new single out." She saw his frown. "Don't you like country music?"

Edward shrugged. "I've never listened to it much. I mostly listen to classical or jazz."

"Oh, elevator music," she said, turning back to her menu.

Edward stared at her in disbelief. How could she refer to Mozart and Chopin or Benny Goodman as elevator music? "Don't you ever listen to anything besides country music?"

"Oh, I've listened to some of that classical stuff when I've had trouble falling asleep. It puts me out like a light." She frowned at him. "Don't look so shocked, Edward. We're different people. We don't like the same things. Come to think of it, I can't think of anything we agree on." She grinned. "Except horror movies. We both love horror movies."

Jack Harris, the owner of the restaurant, approached the table to take their order. Edward was the first to speak. "I'll have the chicken-fried steak, Jack," he said, giving him an award-winning smile. "I hear it's the best in ten counties."

Jack beamed at the compliment, and Maribeth couldn't keep from smiling. She had to give Edward credit for one thing. He certainly could charm folks.

Hours later Maribeth slipped her key into the lock on her front door and pushed it open. The cats didn't make a mad dash for the door, so they were probably curled up on the couch asleep, she thought as she turned around to find Edward standing close behind her. "I . . . uh, had a good time," she said. "I'm sorry you didn't like the movies."

He looked surprised. "How did you know?"

"You snored through both of them." She wasn't about to tell him she'd spent much of that time staring at him, inhaling his after-shave and letting her knee brush against his.

Edward chuckled softly, knowing he'd been found out. When she made a move for the door, he stopped her. "Stay out here for a minute," he said, wondering why she didn't invite him in. He reached around and pulled the door to her apartment closed. A gentle breeze rustled through the trees and played with the curls at her shoulder. He knew the strands would feel like silk if he ran his fingers through them. She was staring at him, he noticed, her expression full of questions.

He had to tell her about his feelings or go insane trying to hide them. He hadn't felt this anxious with a female since high school. He'd been with models and senators' daughters and women executives, but none of them had evoked the kinds of feelings this simple yet outspoken woman did. And none of them had ever looked so lovely in the moonlight.

"Maribeth, I don't know if you realize it, but I'm beginning to care for you." It came out stilted, as if he'd read it from a script. How could one woman have such an effect on him? Edward wondered. She, on the other hand, appeared stunned. "I don't know what's happening between us, but I like it and don't want it to stop," he blurted out. If she was the type that went for smooth-talking men, he would rate low on the scale. But he couldn't think straight when he was around her. He raised his hands slowly to her face and cupped her cheeks, no longer able to keep from touching her. Not even his imagination could have prepared him for how soft her skin was. Her lips parted in surprise, and he felt his own being drawn to them with a force that took his breath away. He lowered his head slowly, and for one agonizing heartbeat searched her eyes. They were soft and ready for love. His lips descended.

Maribeth tensed slightly as his mouth touched hers, and her pulse thumped an erratic message in her throat. Edward kissed her gently but firmly, grasping her chin with one hand and tilting her face so as to give him better access to her lips. When he broke the kiss and moved to her throat, she released her breath and realized she'd been holding it for a long time, perhaps all evening, waiting for him to kiss her again. She snaked her arms around his neck and pulled him closer. His scent surrounded her like a sensuous cloud. His lips moved to her ear and her flesh prickled in delight. He traced the delicate line of her jaw before raining dewy kisses on her eyelids. Her knees threatened to give beneath her. Her head fell against his broad chest. She could smell the newness of his shirt as she rubbed her cheek against the fabric.

"You're beautiful," he whispered in a voice that caressed her.

She shook her head slightly, trying to rouse her befuddled brain. "You shouldn't be saying these things to me, Edward. I'm an employee. You're my boss, remember?"

He chuckled. "Why is it you only acknowledge that fact *outside* of the office?" He pulled her tighter against him. "That doesn't mean anything to me, and I sincerely doubt it means anything to you." His hands slid down her arms and captured her firmly around the waist. "I've wanted to hold you and kiss you from the moment we met," he confessed, "and it was worth almost having my bank robbed just to be tied up with you in that closet."

"Edward—" For the first time in her life Maribeth was speechless.

"Invite me in," he prodded gently, his breath warm and sweet on her face. He kissed her nose and eyelids as he spoke, and his lips were soft as dandelion fluff on her skin.

Maribeth knew she would be courting danger if she did. The silken tone of his voice made his suggestion sound so loving and natural, so easy to oblige. It was deliciously tempting. "You're moving too fast for me,

Edward," she said, almost gasping for breath. "I don't know how they do things in New York, but out here we move a bit slower."

He sighed in her hair. "Okay, Maribeth. I'm prepared to wait. But don't make me wait too long. I don't think I could stand it." He gave her one final kiss and turned for the stairs, already anticipating the cold shower he was going to have to take once he got home. He didn't look back, couldn't look back, or his resolve would melt instantly.

Maribeth was trembling from head to toe as she let herself into her apartment. She leaned against the door in the darkness, trying to get her swirling thoughts under control. A minute later there was a light knock at the door, and she jumped. She opened it, knowing it must be Edward. She found herself looking into the eyes of Moss Gentry.

Four

Maribeth stared in disbelief. "What are you doing here?" she demanded, switching on all the lights.

Moss looked wounded. "Aren't you going to invite me in?" he asked, moving past her anyway. She could smell the whiskey on his breath. "That was quite a performance you and lover boy put on out there. You're real impressed with his fancy clothes and that snazzy car he drives, aren't you?"

"You're drunk, Moss, and you don't know what you're talking about."

"I know exactly what I'm talking about. You're the only friend Edward Spears has in this town. He needs you right now because you're his only hope of getting close to the folks here. He's using you, Maribeth, and you're just dumb enough to fall for it."

"Please leave," she said tightly.

Moss moved closer. "But he ain't gonna make it here," he said, as though he hadn't heard her. "That bank is going to flop, and when it does, Spears is going to take the first plane back to New York." He looked smug. "And where is that going to leave you?"

"What I choose to do about Edward is none of your business. You have no right—"

"I have every right," he said, taking her by the arms and shaking her. "and you're going to stop seeing him or—"

"Or what?" she demanded. "You'll beat him up? Smash his face in?" She twisted free. "That's the only way you know how to get what you want, isn't it? You're nothing but a big bully, Moss. You've bullied me all your life and I've had it up to here with you." She made a slashing gesture across her throat.

"*You've* had it," he bellowed so loud, Maribeth was certain the neighbors had heard. "How do you think it feels being on the road all week and coming home to find your girl in another man's arms?"

"I am *not* your girl!" she said just as loudly.

Moss slammed his fist on the counter. "Dammit, Maribeth. How many times do I have to tell you? I love you."

Maribeth stared at him in silence. Moss seemed to sag before her. "Moss, let's not say anything more, okay? I'm mad and you're drunk. We'll only end up hurting each other."

"I've been hurting for two years, Maribeth. Ever since you went off to Atlanta. You and I grew up together, Maribeth. We understand each other. You and Spears come from different worlds."

"And I love you, too, Moss," she said softly, "but not in the same way."

"Don't give me that brotherly-love routine," he said sourly.

She turned her back on him. "Please leave, Moss. I'm very tired, and I don't want to rehash this whole thing."

"Okay, I'll leave. But I want you to think about what I said. I'm not going to give you up easily." He slammed the door on his way out.

Maribeth hurried across the room and locked the

door. She should go to bed and forget the conversation that had just taken place, she told herself. But Moss's comment about her and Edward being from different worlds stuck with her. Moss was right, and from now on she was going to have to keep a tight rein on her emotions. It was going to be strictly business with Edward. No more kissing!

"Martha, that was the best meal I've had in months," Edward said two nights later. "And that chocolate cake was out of this world."

Martha Hines beamed at him from across the table. "It's nothing less than you deserve," she said. "Nobody has ever taken the time to show me how to manage a checkbook or work out a budget. I can't thank you enough." She smiled shyly. "I know Melvin thought it was his duty to manage the finances and all, but I can't help but feel a bit angry with him for not teaching me how to do some of it. When he died, I was lost."

"How long were you married?" Edward asked.

"Thirty-five years. We had a good marriage, Melvin and me. The only regret I have is that we couldn't have children. I've always loved children. Some of my friends are grandmothers now. I envy them so."

Edward pondered the thought. "Have you ever thought of going into child-care, Martha? The nursery near town is advertising for part-time help. The money shouldn't interfere with what you're getting from the government." And he knew she needed the cash.

"Do you think they'd hire someone with no experience?"

He smiled. "All you need is two arms and a warm heart."

"Do you think I'd be good at it?" she asked wistfully.

"I think you'd be great at it."

Martha thought about it for a moment. "By golly, I'm going," she said. "Bright and early tomorrow morning."

"Good for you." Edward pulled his chair away from the table. "I need to get home. Thanks again for a wonderful meal."

She followed him to the door. "I hope this means I'm forgiven for that awful scene in your office."

"It's already forgotten." He gave her a warm look. "You won't be getting any more pink slips from my bank."

"You're very kind, Edward," she said sincerely.

Edward made his way down the steps to his car and waved at Martha one last time before climbing in. As he pulled out of the gravel drive, he sighed. At least there was one person who didn't have his name on her hate list. One person out of a town of five thousand.

When Maribeth arrived at the bank Monday morning, she found Edward sipping coffee in his office and reading *The Wall Street Journal*. "You're going to have to exchange that newspaper for *The Laurel Gazette*," she said.

He glanced up at her and smiled. "I didn't hear you come in." He glanced at his watch. "You're usually not here until nine-fifteen."

"Very funny," she said, knowing he loved to goad her about her habitual tardiness. She noticed how nicely his starched blue dress shirt went with his dark coloring. "Have a nice weekend?" she asked, when in fact, what she really wanted to know was "Why didn't you call?"

"It was okay," he said, noticing how her hair curled beguilingly around her face. He ached to run his fingers through it as he had the other night and kiss those coral stained lips. "How about dinner tonight?" he asked.

"Maribeth was taken by surprise. "Dinner?"

"Sorry. I believe it's referred to as supper around here."

"Why?" She blinked.

He shrugged. He couldn't very well tell her he was crazy about her and looking for any excuse to be with her. She had already told him he was moving too fast. He'd have to think up something better than that. "I thought it would give us a chance to discuss our strategy for getting me better acclimated to the townspeople."

"Oh," she said dully. Business. It figured. "What time?"

He smiled the same smile that always sent her heart fluttering. "Why don't we plan it for six-thirty? That way I'll know to expect you around seven."

She nodded. "I'll be there."

Maribeth turned into the driveway of the two-story Colonial and parked, then wiped her moist palms on her slacks. Lordy, but she was nervous. She studied the house and its surroundings for a moment, noticing the changes that had taken place since Edward had moved in. The house boasted a new coat of white paint, and the shutters had been changed from black to a deep forest-green. Edward's great-grandfather had built the house, she knew, and had passed it down through the family. It was in remarkably good shape for its age. Whether or not Edward was planning to stay, he was at least seeing the house was well cared for.

She sighed and climbed out of the car, chiding herself for being so nervous. She'd had dinner with men in their apartments before. Why should this be any different? You go in, you eat, you help wash the dishes, and you leave. Simple as that. Yes, but this *was* different. She had never before felt the things Edward made her feel—giddy and light-headed and a bit crazy. She looked at the house again. Lights were shining in the windows on the first floor, giving the place a warm, welcoming appearance. She took a deep breath and made her way up the walk. Besides, this was business. Strictly business.

She rang the doorbell and waited, scrutinizing her appearance. Her khaki slacks were ironed to perfection, and her knit pullover neat and clean. Her loafers had been polished to a brilliance. Knowing Edward's fastidious nature where clothes were concerned, she'd decided against her usual dress of jeans, sweatshirt, and sneakers. The door swung open and Edward stood there, looking at her in a way that made her glad she'd dressed up. He, on the other hand, was wearing a pair of recently purchased jeans, a cotton jersey, and worn sneakers.

"You dressed up," he said in surprise.

"You didn't," she said, equally surprised.

"Should I change?"

She shook her head. "No, you look comfortable." And downright sexy, she added to herself.

He motioned for her to come in. "I was afraid you would back out," he said as she passed through the door. His gaze traveled the length of her, giving extra attention to her round bottom and trim waist. He caught the faint scent of her perfume and closed his eyes briefly, knowing it was going to be an impossible evening. How could he think when the smell of soap and honeysuckle filled the air?

"Why would I back out?" she asked casually. "Like you said, it will give us a chance to discuss our strategy. I already have one idea that might work." She saw the living room and stopped dead in her tracks.

Edward waited for a response. "Do you like it? Most of the furniture came out of my Manhattan apartment."

"It's beautiful," she said sincerely, but that didn't

mean she liked it. It only emphasized how vastly different she was from Edward in everything, including taste. The living room looked like something she would expect to find in a New York apartment—ultramodern, plenty of chrome and glass, and odd-shaped lacquered chairs. The chintz drapes his grandmother had used had been replaced with miniblinds. She couldn't help but wonder what had happened to the plump sofa and chairs as well.

"You don't like it," he said dully. "I can tell by the look on your face."

"It hardly matters what I think. You're the one who has to live here."

He didn't answer. It *did* matter. He had wanted her to like it, to feel comfortable in his home. Then he remembered her apartment, the warm and cozy feelings it evoked. Suddenly his living room looked cold and sterile. "Come into the kitchen," he said, determined not to let their decorating differences interfere with his plans for a wonderful evening. "You can talk to me while I finish dinner."

"It smells like something Italian," she said.

"Lasagna." He guided her toward the kitchen with his hand at the small of her back, and Maribeth let him, although she knew the way. He ached to slide his hand down over the swell of her hips. "Do you like it?"

"Like what?" she asked vaguely, very much aware of the warmth of his hand through her knit pullover.

"Lasagna."

She laughed to hide her embarrassment. "Oh, yes. I can easily eat my weight in it." She entered the kitchen and smiled, seeing that many of his grandmother's belongings remained.

"I haven't gotten around to decorating this room yet," he said. "I kind of like it the way it is." He motioned for her to take a seat on one of the stools at the counter. "Can I get you something to drink? A glass of wine? Coke?"

She shook her head. "I'll wait until dinner. What can I do to help?"

He was surprised by her offer of assistance. Most women he'd known were content to sit and let him do all the work. "You can set the table if you like," he said, going back to preparing the salad. "Do you want to eat in the dining room or here in the kitchen?"

"This room is fine." She gave him another smile. "It was always my favorite," she said, glancing at the round oak table and chairs. An antique vase sat in the center, filled with an assortment of artificial flowers and greenery.

He nodded. "I know what you mean. I can still remember sitting with my grandfather at that table eating pancakes. My grandmother made the best in the world." He picked up a grater and began shredding a carrot.

"She also made the best chocolate-chip cookies," Maribeth said. "She always made tons of them at Christmas." Maribeth rounded the counter to stand beside Edward. "Where do you keep your silverware?" she asked. He pulled open a drawer and his elbow accidentally brushed the side of her breast. She jumped as though she'd received an electric shock.

"Sorry," he muttered, wishing she weren't so jumpy.

She nodded, but her cheeks burned as she reached into the drawer and selected what silverware they would need. Why had she overreacted like that? she asked herself. She slipped past him, careful not to let any part of her body touch his. She carried the silverware to the table and put it in its proper order. "Where do you keep the plates?" she asked as soon as she was finished. She tried to keep her voice light.

Edward was in the process of dicing a tomato and couldn't let go. "Right over my head." He waited until she was beside him, then ducked. "Go ahead and open the cabinet," he said.

Maribeth reached over his head and opened it. She scooted a bit closer and stretched on tiptoe to get to the plates and salad bowls, unaware just how close she and Edward were. Edward sucked in his breath sharply as, unbeknownst to her, her breasts came within inches of his face, as she selected the dishes she needed. He could only stare. Her breasts looked lush and ripe beneath the clinging knit sweater. Perfectly rounded. Begging to be caressed. He could just imagine the smooth texture, see the milky-white color, feel the quivering nipples between his fingertips. The urge to bury his face in her softness was so strong, he gritted his teeth and jerked his head up with the force of a man being chased by demons.

Pain sliced through his skull as it made contact with the corner of the cabinet door. He muttered a curse, certain he had just knocked his brains out.

Maribeth almost dropped the dishes when she heard the painful thud. "Are you okay?" she asked worriedly, setting the dishes on the counter. "Where does it hurt?"

He dropped the knife and tomato and groped for a dishtowel to dry his hands. "Right here," he answered, bending over slightly and pointing to a spot.

Maribeth slid her fingers through his hair and searched for the knot that was certain to appear. "Does this hurt?" she asked, pressing the area he'd pointed to.

He winced. "Of course, it hurts. Why? Is it supposed to feel good?"

A laugh bubbled out. "Sorry," she said. "Dumb question. Hold still while I get some ice."

"Don't bother. Nothing is going to help." He attempted to smile. "Unless you have a bullet I can bite. You didn't happen to bring one of your six-shooters with you tonight, did you?"

She gave him a dirty look as she hurried to the refrigerator. "I don't carry a gun," she said, throwing open the freezer door. She pulled out an ice tray and in a matter of seconds had a homemade ice pack. "Sit on one of those stools so I can put this on your head."

"This really isn't necessary, you know." He saw the look of determination on her face and realized it was useless to argue. Once she got her mind set on something, there was no turning back. He sat down on a stool and hitched his heels on the bottom rung. His knees were bent and his thighs parted as he situated himself comfortably. Maribeth, whose only concern was getting the swelling down on his head, moved between his thighs without a second thought and pressed the ice pack against the growing lump on his skull.

Edward froze. Her nearness, the intimate position, was almost his undoing. She moved closer to get a better look at the bump and he held his breath, his expression tight with strain. Her perfume, the smell of soap, tormented him. His eyes zoomed in on her breasts once more. He was right back where he'd started. Didn't she know what she did to him? Had she no idea how crazy she made him from wanting her?

"Does it still hurt?"

"Uh-huh." His tone was husky. He was hurting all right, but not from the lump on his head.

At the strange sound of his voice, Maribeth glanced down at him. All at once it hit her, the intimate position they were in. Her lips parted in surprise and she jumped back, dropping the ice pack. It fell to the floor and the cubes rolled from the cloth. Before she could make another move, Edward snaked his arms around her waist, pulling her back to him.

"I like your style of doctorin'," he said, a grin spreading across his face. "Could we check out your bedside manner now?"

Maribeth took a quick breath. Why was she so surprised to find herself in his arms? she wondered. She had been waiting for it to happen. It was inevitable.

For a moment they merely stared at each other, the air alive with anticipation. She could feel the sexual magnetism that had drawn them together in the beginning. Now it was as threatening as a live wire. And she was powerless to resist. Very slowly Edward pulled her face to his. She felt the slightest whisper of his warm breath against her cheek before his lips claimed hers.

His kiss was slow and thorough, and it shattered her senses like a raging storm and sent them swirling. All coherent thought ceased. His mouth moved over hers expertly as he anchored her face between his hands. Her knees threatened to give. He tightened his grip on her, signalling that he wouldn't let her fall. He broke the kiss, and his lips reappeared at the hollow of her throat. Maribeth did not know a man's mouth could feel so good.

Her head fell against his shoulder; she was in a daze. Still, she could feel his heart hammering wildly, and his broad chest heaved with every breath he took. She ached to slide her hands beneath his shirt and learn the mossy texture of his chest, to run her fingers lightly over the hard muscles across his shoulders and back. And she didn't want to stop there. That thought frightened her. "Edward, we shouldn't—"

"We have to." His voice was thick. "You know I'm crazy about you."

"But I'm not . . . uh, ready. And there are so many unanswered questions." Like how long he planned to hang around, she thought.

He sighed heavily, his lips in her hair. "Is it Moss?"

"No."

"Then what?"

"Well . . ." She paused. "I keep wondering what's going to happen if your bank doesn't make it."

He frowned. "You don't have much confidence in me, do you?"

"It's not that, Edward. But I have to think of myself.

You say you care for me, but if things don't work out for you here, where does that leave me?"

"You could always go back to New York with me."

She shook her head. "I wouldn't last two days in that place."

He slipped his hand beneath the curtain of hair on her neck and stroked her skin. "Maribeth, why don't we worry about what's happening right now and let the future take care of itself? I'm doing everything in my power to make the bank a success, not just for you but for me as well."

"What do you mean?"

He looked into her eyes. "I kind of like it here. I enjoy waking up in the morning to the sounds of birds chirping instead of listening to traffic and sirens and horns blowing. I like being able to walk out back in my bathrobe and drink my first cup of coffee while watching the squirrels scramble across the yard and up the trees." He smiled. "At first, I thought all the people here were slow, then I realized they're not slow, they're just not in a hurry. It's made me take a long look at myself and wonder, why have I always been in such a rush? This place, this life, has substance, Maribeth, something I never found in New York."

"But won't you miss it?" she asked.

"I'm sure I'll miss the shows and the nightclubs. But I've found just as much pleasure working on this house or reading a book by the fireplace."

She was surprised. "Did you paint the house yourself?"

"Uh-huh." He grinned. "I had no idea what I was getting myself into at the time, all the scraping I had to do beforehand. I've never done anything before that I was really proud of. But I was very proud when I finished."

"You should be. It looks nice."

"I'm learning to do all sorts of things. And I'm going to have a garden this year as soon as I can figure out how to use a tiller."

She laughed. "I'll show you. I'll even help you plant your garden if you like."

He squeezed her gently. "I like."

"Only if you promise not to burn the lasagna."

He jumped up suddenly, remembering it was time to take the dish out of the oven. "See what you do to me, lady?" he asked, stuffing both hands into thick pot-holders. He opened the oven door and was relieved to see the meal was not burned.

They conversed easily over dinner. Edward told her of his life in New York, and she told him what it was like growing up in Laurel. Their lives had been so different, she realized, they might as well have been raised on different planets. Afterward she told him there was a Chamber of Commerce meeting on Wednesday, and he agreed he should attend. But it was obvious neither of them had their minds on what they were saying. Edward's eyes caressed her face, her hair, her throat, and ultimately landed on her breasts. She could feel them swell beneath her sweater at his intimate look. They had reached a turning point in their relationship, she knew. He had been content to be her employer and her friend, and he'd tried to give her time to sort out her feelings for Moss. But now it was obvious he wanted more. Much more.

After dinner he built a roaring fire in the fireplace in the living room and suggested they drink their coffee in front of it. "Have a seat," he said to her, pointing to the sofa.

She hesitated. "Could we just sit on the floor?" she asked, glancing doubtfully at the vanilla-colored fabric on the sofa. But the carpet wasn't much better, she realized once she sat down. It was a champagne color. She'd heard from Carol that Edward had ordered the nubby-textured carpet through Dan, the same carpet that had been used in the White House and cost ninety-five dollars a square yard. She was trying to figure out what it must have cost to do the entire room when he joined her. She caught him staring at her. "Dinner was excellent," she said, feeling the need to say something. "Next time I'll cook." It was out before she thought about it. She had just asked the man for a date, and she didn't know if she was going to make it through this one. Why was she always so tense when she was around him?

"I'd love to," he said. "When?"

"When?" she repeated, stupefied by his quick acceptance. "Uh, well, how about Thursday night? Unless you're busy, of course. If you're busy, we can do it another night." Like in a year or two, she thought. When she learned how to cook and he didn't make her a nervous wreck just by being around.

"Thursday is fine." He studied her for a moment. "Are you okay?"

"I'm fine," she said breathlessly. It was a bold-faced lie. She had a terrible case of the jitters.

"I know what you need." He was already on his feet. "I'm going to get you a glass of brandy."

"Oh, no, I'm fine. Really." It was useless to argue. He was halfway to the kitchen.

A moment later he was back, carrying two snifters of brandy. "Here, drink this," he said. "It'll help you relax." He held out one of the glasses.

She reached for it. "Just a tiny bit," she said anxiously. "I'm driving home, remember?"

"If it goes to your head, I'll drive you home." He gave her a sexy smile. "Unless you'd rather stay here."

His words hit her like a freight train. She downed the drink in one gulp. The fiery liquid blazed a path to her stomach and made her eyes water. She coughed and sputtered for a full minute before she gained control of herself.

Edward gave her a couple of firm slaps on the back. He looked amused. "Heck, Gunsmoke, if I had known you drank like a regular cowhand, I would have carried the bottle in with me." He held out his glass. "Have another?"

"Uh, no." She swallowed again, praying the liquid would stop burning before long. She placed the glass on the coffee table with a trembling hand. Edward took a sip of his drink and set it on the table beside hers. Then, much to Maribeth's surprise, he walked around the room switching off lights. Her questioning eyes never left him. He, on the other hand, went about the whole thing as though it were perfectly normal. Must be the way they did things in New York, she thought. He sat beside her.

"I thought we could lie on the floor and watch the fire," he said, handing her one of the throw pillows he'd grabbed from the couch. "This is probably going to be the last one of the season." He disregarded the look of caution in her eyes as he stretched out in front of the fire and tucked a pillow under his head. He closed his eyes and sighed, as though perfectly content.

He also seemed oblivious to her. Maribeth didn't know whether to feel relieved or insulted.

The fire cast a soft glow throughout the room. Shadows danced eerily in the corners, but in front of the fire it was warm and cozy. Maribeth studied Edward in the firelight. His legs looked endless in the tight-fitting jeans, his thighs hard and lean and muscular. His shirt stretched nicely across his wide chest and stomach. He looked sexy as heck lying there.

She wanted him.

Maribeth drank in the handsome face and strong jaw, aching to touch it, to run her fingers across his lips. One caress, one word, was all he needed. He was waiting for her to make the decision. She bit her bottom lip, racked with indecision. Part of her wanted to flee, to run as far away from him as she could. Moss's warning rang loudly in her mind. But another part of her wanted to stay and share with Edward all the intimacies between a man and woman. She wanted to know the tastes and textures of him.

She wanted to do things to him she'd never done before, things she'd only read about. That thought put a rosy blush on her cheeks.

But then what? She would naturally fall in love with him. And what if he left? What if he grew bored with the simple life or the people that lived here? Worse, what if he grew bored with her? He had said he was crazy about her, but what did that prove? She was crazy about Snicker's candy bars and buttered popcorn and scented bubble baths, but she could live without them. She squeezed her eyes closed. What if the bank failed? Her heart sank. There were just too many what ifs. Even though Moss's motives had been selfish, he had clearly pointed those contingencies out to her.

Very slowly she raised herself from the floor and made her way toward the front door. Her purse was lying on one of the lacquered chairs, and she grabbed it. She placed her hand on the doorknob.

"Maribeth?"

She turned around and found Edward hiked up on one elbow, watching her. "It's getting late," she said, her voice reaching an odd pitch.

"Don't go," he said gently. "Stay with me for a while." Even in the dim light his eyes compelled her.

It sounded so simple, so tempting; yet she knew one kiss was all it would take. She could just imagine them lying naked in each other's arms, basking in the warmth of the fire. Edward's hair-roughened body against hers would be sheer heaven, Maribeth thought. Would he make love to her right there on the carpet or would he carry her into the bedroom? She squinched her eyes closed, trying to erase the sensual pictures she was creating in her mind. Already her bones felt as though they were turning to mush under his coaxing look. Her resolve was fading.

But tonight wouldn't last forever. Tomorrow would be a new day, fresh with doubt. "I can't," she said simply, honestly.

"Running from me isn't going to solve a thing, Maribeth. I think you want me as badly as I want you. Sooner or later it's going to happen between us."

She was out the door before she could change her mind.

Edward continued to sit before the fire long after he'd heard Maribeth drive away. He had thought of running after her but decided against it. He had wanted to pin her down on the floor and kiss her senseless, until all her fears faded, but he wouldn't allow himself to do that. From what little he could pick up about her and Moss's relationship, Maribeth had been bullied long enough. Perhaps that was why she was so outspoken now. He didn't want to force her into intimacy; he wanted her to come to him on her own. He had felt her staring at him for a long time before she ran out the door, and he would have given anything to know her thoughts.

He stood and picked up his brandy and drained it. He carried the glass into the kitchen and set it down before letting himself out the back door. He stood on the small patio out back and gazed at the clear starlit sky. He'd never stopped to look at the sky when he lived in New York other than to gaze out his apartment window at the neighboring skyscrapers or the horizon of city lights. He'd never listened to the constant chirping of crickets or heard the hollow bass sound of a bullfrog, other than the short time he'd spent with his grandparents. He'd chased lightning bugs in the backyard and was amazed at the way they illuminated and disappeared before he could get his hands on them. His grandfather had sat on this very patio, cranking the handle on a metal container that made ice cream. He'd explained to Edward that only the male crickets made the chirping sounds by rubbing their front wings against their back ones. Somewhere along the line of his chaotic life, he'd forgotten these things, and now that he'd found them again, he wanted to share them with someone else. Maribeth.

He was falling in love with Maribeth Bradford.

Edward continued to gaze at the heavens, but all he saw was her face. He wanted her so badly in that instant that he drew his hands into fists at his sides. And some instinct told him she wanted him equally as much. Yet she remained elusive. What was he fighting against? he wondered. In the beginning he'd thought it was Moss. Now he was beginning to think it was the bank. She was afraid he would fail. That thought made him frown. The person he cared for most dearly had no faith in him.

How long he stood out there and stared at the dark sky and listened to the sounds, he wasn't sure. When he realized he was shivering from the night air, he went back into the house and began turning off the lights. He climbed into bed thirty minutes later and stared into the darkness a long time before falling asleep.

Five

Maribeth eyed the group of businessmen and -women that formed the local chapter of the Chamber of Commerce as she poured coffee for Edward and herself into small plastic cups. Nell Smith, the local baker, was carrying trays of strawberry tarts made fresh that morning and offering them to people. She stopped beside Maribeth and Edward, and neither of them had to be coaxed.

"Well, look who's here!" a feminine voice sang out.

Maribeth didn't have to look to know the voice belonged to Twyla McGregor. She winced mentally. Twyla chased everything in pants. It didn't matter that she was married and had four kids and an insanely jealous husband who followed her everywhere. "Hello, Twyla," Maribeth said coolly.

"So this is the fancy new banker I've been hearing all about," Twyla said in a voice as thick as Karo syrup. "Aren't you going to introduce us?" She tilted her dark head provocatively.

Maribeth made the introductions. "Twyla and her husband," she said, emphasizing the word *husband*, "own McGregor Furniture."

Twyla put out a delicate well-manicured hand and Edward took it. "So nice to meet you, Mr. Spears," she drawled.

"Call me Edward," he said politely.

"I've been wanting to meet you for the longest time, Edward," she said, "but Maribeth has been so stingy with you. I *do* hope we can become friends. *Good* friends," she added, still grasping Edward's hand tightly in hers. "I've been wanting to talk to you about moving my bank account. George closed our accounts when your grandfather passed away. By the way, I am *so* sorry about your grandfather. He was such a good man."

And probably the only one you never made a pass at, Maribeth thought, wondering how a woman could talk so long without stopping to catch her breath. Twyla reminded her of a black widow spider.

". . . and it's such a bother to have to drive clear over to the next town to do our banking."

"I'm sure it is, Mrs. McGregor."

"Twyla."

"Why don't you come into the bank one day and we'll talk about it?" he suggested. "I'm sure you'll find our rates attractive."

"I *know* I will."

Maribeth gazed from one to the other, thinking she could very well become ill. Twyla looked at Edward as if he were the cherry on top of a great big ice-cream sundae. "Would you two excuse me?" she said dully.

"Certainly, dear," Twyla answered, never taking her eyes off Edward.

Maribeth glared at the two of them as she made her way back to the coffeepot. She was giving serious thought to dumping a cup of coffee on Twyla's head when Dan McCloy walked up. "Hi, Dan," she muttered. "Want some coffee?"

"No thanks." he followed her gaze. "I see Twyla is up to her old tricks."

"So what else is new?" Maribeth said crossly, and reached for a clean plastic cup. "Men stick to Twyla like ticks to a hound dog."

"Uh-oh," Dan said. "Don't look now, but you're not going to believe who just walked through the front door."

Maribeth's eyes swept across the room to the front door and gasped. "Moss! What's he doing here? He doesn't attend these meetings." She looked at Dan. "Does he?"

"I've never seen him at one before. He's not a member."

Maribeth pressed her lips together in irritation as Moss smiled and headed in their direction. "He's just coming to make trouble, dammit."

"Now, calm down, Maribeth. We don't know that."

"Why isn't he on the road, for Pete's sake?"

"Hi, Moss," Dan said, reaching out to shake the taller man's hand.

Moss nodded and shook hands with Dan, then glanced around the room. "Oh, I see our new banker is here," he said, his eyes coming to a halt on Edward and Twyla. "Looks to me like he's trying to build a little interest." He nudged Dan. "Get it? Interest?" He threw his head back and laughed.

"Moss, what are you doing here?" Maribeth demanded.

Moss looked truly wounded. "I just thought I'd drop in and see what goes on at these meetings, that's all."

"Oh, no," Dan said. "Twyla's husband is heading their way, and he looks mad enough to chomp steel with his bare teeth."

Moss grinned. "I'm going to enjoy this."

"I think we'd better get over there, Dan," Maribeth said, grabbing his arm. "You know how mean George can get." She dragged Dan toward Twyla and Edward while Moss laughed in the background. She and Dan reached them about the same time George did.

"Twyla!" George McGregor stood directly behind his wife. She jumped at the sound of his voice.

"Oh, good heavens, George," she said, her hand flying to her throat. "You scared the dickens out of me."

Maribeth went into action. "Hello, George," she said, hurriedly. "Have you met our new banker? This is Edward Spears."

George muttered a reply and stuck his hand out for a brief shake. He turned to his wife. "The meeting is about to begin. It's time we found our seats." It wasn't a suggestion; it was an order. Twyla merely nodded and followed like a dutiful wife.

"Well, isn't that just dandy?" Maribeth said to Edward as soon as George and Twyla were out of hearing range. Dan had gone in search of a strawberry tart. "I bring you to a meeting to introduce you to the business community and you try to pick up a married woman."

Edward looked surprised. "You think I was trying to pick her up?"

"It certainly looked that way to me," Moss said, coming up to stand beside them.

"You stay out of this, Moss," Maribeth said as he and Edward exchanged dark glances, then she spun around and walked away.

Moss shrugged. "Sorry, old fellow, but it looks like you lose." He started to follow Maribeth, but stopped. "By the way, I wouldn't mess with that McGregor woman. Her husband will tear your face off." He winked. "I speak from experience."

Maribeth found a seat in the back row. Without a word Edward and Dan joined her, sitting on either side. Moss, she noticed, sat in the front row next to Bart Gentry, his uncle.

Bart Gentry stood up and called the group to order. "I

make a motion we discuss the new mall that has just opened in the next town," he said, and someone seconded it.

Maribeth tried to concentrate on the discussion about the new mall, but her thoughts centered on Edward. What was wrong with her? she wondered. One minute she was determined to avoid him and the next she was fighting mad simply because he'd spoken to another woman. Perhaps he'd been trying to win Twyla over with his charm so she and her husband would bring their business back to his bank. And he could certainly be charming if he wanted, Maribeth thought. He had almost charmed her into his bed the other night. She was thankful he hadn't mentioned it. She sighed. It was a no-win situation with Edward. As long as she concerned herself with his personal life, which included getting him involved in the community, her heart was going to pay.

"We're going to have to think of a way to save our little town," Bart said louder than necessary, startling Maribeth from her thoughts. "If people start driving to the mall to do their shopping, Laurel is going to die."

There was a nod of heads. Several suggestions were made, none of them very good, but Bart made sure the secretary jotted them down. Edward raised his hand and Bart gave him the floor.

Edward stood. "I realize I'm the newest member and all," he began, giving them a smile that made Maribeth's heart beat faster, "but I've got just as much at stake here as the rest of you. If this town dies, so will my bank." He paused a moment. "I propose we fight fire with fire as the saying goes and build our own mall."

A hush filled the room. Maribeth felt her own mouth fall open in disbelief. Even Dan looked puzzled. What could Edward be thinking? she wondered, feeling her face grow hot. She was embarrassed, not only for herself but for him. Suddenly there was a loud laugh from the front row. Moss stood up, grinning broadly. "Excuse me, but did he say we should build our own mall?" he asked. He looked at the group and shook his head as though he couldn't believe his own ears. Maribeth wanted to claw his eyes out. "Where would we put it, for heaven's sake? In a cow pasture?" Several people laughed.

Bart took over. "Sit down, Moss. You're not a member, and you don't have any say-so." Bart scratched his head as though trying to figure out if Edward was serious or not. "We ain't got that kind of money, Mr. Spears." He gave Edward an apologetic smile. "I realize we don't look like much compared to what you got in New York City, but this is the best—"

"Please let me finish," Edward said, his dark eyes shooting darts at Moss's laughing ones. "I'm not suggesting we actually build from the ground up. All I'm suggesting is we merely revamp our shopping community, make it more attractive to our customers."

"Revamp?" Moss said. "What the hell does that mean?"

"I told you to sit down, Moss," Bart said. "If you've got personal troubles, take them outside. We're trying to run a business meeting."

Moss began to argue. Maribeth had had enough. She got up from her chair and made her way toward the back of the room and out the door, oblivious of Edward's look of surprise. Once out on the street, she stood gasping for air, feeling both humiliated and angry. Why she had ever talked Edward into coming to the meeting was beyond her. He didn't have any business in there. He didn't have any business in Laurel, period. Like Moss had said, they came from different worlds.

It was more than an hour later when Edward walked into the office, wearing a dark frown. "What the hell was that all about?" he asked Maribeth. "Why did you walk out on me like that?"

Maribeth had known he would be mad, but nothing had prepared her for the fierce look of anger in his eyes. "I, uh, had a lot of work to do," she said.

"Do you realize how you made me feel back there? You made me look like a fool."

"No, Edward. You managed to do that on your own."

He continued to glare at her. "Well, if you had bothered to hang around, you would have found out differently. It just so happens that I came up with an idea that was so damn good the whole group agreed. And your good friend Moss couldn't think of anything bad to say about it."

He took a deep breath and tried to calm himself. "I never know if you're for me or against me, Maribeth. I get better treatment from Moss. At least I know where I stand with him. I just can't figure you out, Maribeth."

"I don't think you're going to need my help any further in getting you involved in the community, Edward," she said quietly.

"Does this have anything to do with the McGregor woman?" Hell, he couldn't even remember what the woman looked like.

Maribeth faced him squarely. "I certainly don't have any say in the women you choose to become friends with. My only objection to Twyla is that she's a married woman. Think how the people in this town would feel if you were to . . . if two of you were to . . . well, you know."

He looked both angry and frustrated. "I don't believe this. You've already got me having an illicit affair with a woman I probably wouldn't recognize if I saw again. What's gotten into you, Maribeth?" He studied her for a moment, then planted both hands on her desk and leaned forward. "I think it's time we stopped talking about insignificant matters and concentrate on what's important."

"Such as?"

"Us," he ground out. "One minute you're soft and loving in my arms and the next minute you could give a person frostbite. What is it with you?"

"I don't want to talk about this right now, Edward."

"That's too bad. Because we *are* going to talk about it. You're running scared, aren't you?"

"I don't have the slightest idea what you're talking about."

"You don't fool me with this Annie Oakley act you put on. Deep down you're a frightened little girl. That's the real reason you can't shake off Moss. You're still letting him make some of your decisions for you, aren't you? And he knows it. I can't help but wonder how you made it two years in Atlanta. Who made your decisions for you then?"

"I did!" she said, her cheeks hot with anger. "I'm not a child, Edward. I'm twenty-four years old, and I happen to know what I want out of life. And hopping into bed with you isn't at the top of my list. That's what this conversation is really about, isn't it?" She had struck a nerve. It was obvious by the hardening of his jaw.

Instead of lashing out at her as she would have expected, Edward kept his voice very controlled. "You're afraid of going to bed with me because you know you'll fall in love with me. And you can't risk that, can you? Because you don't have enough faith in me to make a place for myself in this town. I see Moss has schooled you well." He shot her a dark look. "But you know what *really* irks the hell out of me, Maribeth?" He didn't give her a chance to answer. "You were willing to risk your life to save this bank from being robbed. But you can't take a risk on me."

Maribeth merely stared at him for a moment. She didn't know what to say. What *could* she say? "Edward . . ." She paused, shaking her head. "You're moving too fast for me. Confusing me. I need time to sort things out. Right now, I just can't handle a relationship with you."

"Not *can't*," he corrected her. "Won't."

"It's got to be strictly business from now on."

"We haven't had a business relationship since the day we met."

"Then it's time we start. Or I'll have to look for another job."

"Is that a threat?"

She sighed, feeling very close to tears. "No. It's the simple truth."

He studied her for a moment, hating the scared look in her eyes. "Very well. If that's the way you want it." He stalked to his office and slammed the door.

Maribeth went back to her typing. She had to retype a letter five times to get it right, and she prayed that none of the tellers would need her assistance because she couldn't think straight. She had done exactly as she had intended, gained some distance from Edward. That was the only way she could prevent herself from falling in love with him and then risk losing him. She had made the right decision. So why did she feel so miserable?

Maribeth was twenty minutes late for work the next morning. Edward was waiting for her, looking very much like Little Miss Muffet's spider. "I'm sorry I'm late," she began breathlessly, "but my car wouldn't start and—"

"Spare me the excuses, Miss Bradford," he said. "I'm sure you have enough of them to land a spot on *Ripley's Believe It or Not*, but I'm not interested. I trust you'll make up the time during your lunch hour." He ignored the frown she gave him and tossed a confession magazine on her desk. "One of our customers found this in our lobby this morning. Don't you think it's a bit much for the bank?"

Maribeth winced at seeing the cover page, where the title **I Was a Sex-starved Housewife** stood out in bold letters. How the magazine had found its way to the lobby was beyond her. She and the tellers usually kept them well hidden. "I'm sorry," she said. "I'll make sure it doesn't happen again." She saw the stern look in his eyes. "I said I was sorry." He didn't have to get himself in such snit about it.

He nodded and handed her a thick stack of letters. "I'd like these ready for my signature by noon."

She took them and glanced through the pages. There were at least three dozen letters. "Then I suggest you hire another secretary immediately," she answered half jokingly. When he didn't so much as crack a smile, she turned on her heels and tossed them onto her desk. "Very well," she said crisply. "I'll have them ready." She sat at her desk and watched his retreating back and had the sudden childish urge to stick her tongue out at him. So that was how he was going to play it from now on, she thought. Well, she could be just as nasty.

Five minutes later Edward's door opened. "Miss Bradford, did you forget to water the plants in my office again?" he asked. "The leaves are beginning to turn brown, and they need to be snipped."

Maribeth recoiled mentally. How many times had he reminded her to water those dumb plants? She glanced up at him with an apology on her lips but bit it back when she saw the smug look on his face. "Excuse me, Mr. Spears," she said tightly, "but I believe you have confused my duties with that of a horticulturist. I type letters and answer your phone, sir. But I do not feed, water, and snip leaves from plants."

"Forget I asked. I'll water the damn plants myself."

By five-thirty Maribeth was tired of the whole thing and her head was splitting. Somehow, she had managed to complete the stack of letters he'd brought out that morning, but only by skipping her lunch hour. As soon as she'd handed him the stack he'd given her a fresh one. "Slave driver," she muttered under her breath as she cleaned off her desk. She grabbed her purse and hurried out the back door toward her car. She was in no mood to face him.

Maribeth saw that the parking lot was almost deserted, with the exception of Edward's car and the one belonging to the security guard. She walked to her car and climbed in. When she inserted her key into the ignition and turned it, nothing happened. "Damn car," she muttered crossly. It was the battery, she knew. The same thing had happened that morning and she had had to jump-start it with a neighbor's car. She had the battery cables; what she needed at the moment was another car with a working battery. She leaned her head on the steering wheel and sighed in pure frustration. She was not going to resort to tears, she told herself. She was tired and hungry and had a headache and a bum car, but she was determined not to cry about it.

"Having trouble?" a male voice asked.

She looked up and found Edward at her window, an amused look in his eyes. She opened the door and got out, thankful he had not left the office before her. "It's my battery," she said, forgetting her anger at him for the moment. She opened the hood of her car. "I've been meaning to buy a new one, but—" She paused and laughed, gazing skeptically at her old Buick. "What I really need is a new car. I've got jumper cables in the trunk if you wouldn't mind jump-starting me." She unlocked her truck and pulled out a set of cables and carried them around to the front of the car, where Edward was still standing. He hadn't made a move to assist her.

"Well?" she said, giving him a hopeful smile. "Do you mind?"

He didn't return the smile, but folded his arms across his chest. "Miss Bradford, I'm afraid you've confused my duties with that of a mechanic. I do not change spark plugs, do lube jobs, nor do I jump-start automobiles. Now, if you'll excuse me."

Maribeth knew he was still mad at her, but he wouldn't just walk away and leave her stranded, with the nearest gas station two miles away, would he?

She watched in disbelief as he climbed into his car and drove away.

It was after six-thirty when Maribeth arrived home, exhausted and angry. Both cats made a mad dash for her, knowing it was past their dinnertime. After spooning food into their bowls, Maribeth headed straight for the bathroom, where she found a bottle of aspirin in the medicine cabinet. She popped two of them into her mouth and swallowed enough water to make them go down. Darn the man. Who did he think he was, leaving her stranded in the middle of the parking lot? She would have still been standing there if it hadn't been for Mr. Phelps, the security guard, who'd been more than happy to assist her. Of course, Mr. Phelps was a southern gentleman, Edward a New Yorker. That said it all.

Before long Maribeth's headache had lessened, if not her sour disposition. Now that their stomachs were satisfied, Raisin Bran and Corn Flake were curled on the sofa sleeping. Maribeth took a hot shower, then slipped into a pair of cutoff jeans and T-shirt, and pulled on a pair of knee socks. She let her damp hair hang around her shoulders, and before long her natural curl began to dry into thick waves and attractive curlicues at her face. Her stomach growled loudly, reminding her she hadn't eaten all day. She was ravenous. But when she opened the door to her refrigerator, all she found was a half gallon of orange juice, two carrots, and a brown, wilted head of lettuce. Her cabinets proved equally bare with the exception of a moldy loaf of bread. She closed the door and leaned against the cabinet, trying to think when she'd last set foot in a grocery store other than to buy coffee and cat food.

She felt like crying. Or throwing something. But food and fatigue weren't the only reasons. It was Edward. She hadn't realized what an important part he played in her life until the last couple of days. She loved going to work every day, knowing he'd be there. She enjoyed sharing little tidbits of her life with him and listening as he shared some of his own. They had laughed together and worked together. They had shared fear. They had shared desire.

Giving it up was like giving up a piece of herself.

She sighed and plodded toward her bedroom, determined to forget her troubles and go to bed. She had just reached her bedroom when she heard a knock at her door. She hurried to the kitchen, where she paused at her door long enough to slide the chair free and flip the lock open on the dead bolt. She was surprised to find Edward on the other side, wearing jeans and a western-style shirt.

He took one look at her and laughed. "Does this mean you forgot I was coming to dinner tonight?" he asked. "This *is* Thursday, isn't it?"

Her mouth flew open. She'd been so angry with him, she'd forgotten all about having invited him. "Well, I . . . uh . . ."

"A simple yes will do."

They merely stared at each other for a moment. Maribeth thought she detected a trace of humor in his eyes. He looked so different now from when she'd given him such a hard time over his plants. Lord, how *did* the man manage to work with her? She felt the beginnings of a smile on her lips and before she knew it they were both laughing.

"I guess I did forget," she said, apologetically.

"That's funny. I thought for sure you would be feeding me your old battery." His look sobered. "I drove by the bank three times to make sure Phelps got it started for you."

"You did? I never saw you."

"I made certain of it," he said, grinning.

She gave him a stern look. "You'll have to admit that was a mean thing you did. Leaving me stranded like that. Not to mention defenseless."

"Maribeth Bradford defenseless?" His eyes caressed her face before dropping to her T-shirt. She wasn't wearing a bra. Why did she do these things to him? "I pity the poor soul who would try to take advantage of you," he said on a lighter note, although it was difficult to keep from staring at the buds pressing against the fabric of her limp shirt. His look became almost tender as his gaze crept back to her face, which was so very pretty, even without makeup. "I'm sorry," he finally said. "I was angry and couldn't help myself. Forgive me?"

She held her breath. How could she not forgive him when he looked at her like that? His eyes were the color of cocoa, dark and rich and full of expression. His lips tempted her. "I'll forgive you," she said breathlessly, "if you'll take me somewhere to eat. I'm starving."

"I figured you would be," he said, wanting to slip his fingers through the damp ringlets that cascaded over her shoulders. "So I brought dinner." He motioned for her to wait as he hurried down to his car. He returned a minute later carrying a large flat box. "I hope you like pizza," he said, following her inside. "I had to drive to the next town for it."

"I love it. Even more than lasagna, as a matter of fact."

"Uh-oh." He glanced at the large box skeptically. "Maybe I should have ordered two."

She slapped him playfully on the arm as he set the box on the table. "I hope you don't mind drinking orange juice with it," she said, taking the carton of juice out of the refrigerator. "It's all I have."

Edward looked into the empty refrigerator. "Why don't you ever buy food? Surely I'm paying you enough. How do you live without eating?"

"Oh, I eat," she said. "Sometimes I drop by the J&M Restaurant or go to my parents' house for dinner. Other times I stop at the store for a frozen dinner." She shrugged. "Why should I buy food when I don't know how to cook?"

"You don't know how to cook *anything*?" he asked in disbelief.

"I can cook hot dogs. And cornbread."

"That sounds like a wonderful combination."

"Oh, don't get me wrong," she said, pouring two glasses of orange juice. "I can cook anything frozen or in a can." She went back for the plates and handed them to him. He lifted two thick slices of pizza onto the plates.

"Why hasn't someone thought of opening a pizza parlor here?"

She shrugged. "You could always bring it up at the next Chamber of Commerce meeting," she said, taking the plate he offered her. She gave him a coy look. "Have you decided to let me in on the great ideas you had at the last meeting about trying to save our town with that new mall?"

He gave her a stern look. "I don't know." Actually he was still hurt over her walking out on him. "Maybe if you ask me nicely."

"Pleeeeze," she said.

He couldn't help but smile. Damn, he'd missed her. "Okay, I'll tell you. All I suggested was that people paint the outside of their stores the same color or use the same color scheme. You know, like painting it in

Williamsburg colors? You'll have to admit, this town could use a facelift. I also suggested we all put up matching awnings and big flowerpots, close the main shopping area to traffic, and put parking areas in the back. That way we could set out benches, even an outside café. Then when it's finished, we could have a grand reopening—balloons for the kids, hot dogs, all the frills—and announce it on the radio. Bart suggested we hire an interior decorator to help us. A lot of folks also said it was high time they made a few changes on the insides of their stores as well."

"Edward, that's a wonderful idea."

He shrugged. "Everybody else seemed to think so. See what you missed by leaving early?" He tried to sound casual and not let her know how hurt he'd been.

She dropped her gaze. "Edward, I'm really sorry about that."

"Eat your pizza," he said, wanting to drop the subject.

They talked about nonessential matters while Maribeth consumed four slices of pizza. Their fight was forgotten. Edward offered her another slice of pizza, but she leaned back in her chair and groaned. "I haven't eaten this much since you plied me with lasagna."

He watched her wipe her mouth with a napkin. Even without lipstick her mouth was the color of peaches and, he knew, would taste just as sweet. He reached over and took one slender hand in his. "Does this mean we're friends again?" he asked hopefully. "And we don't have to go through that nonsense at the office?"

Maribeth nodded. She slipped her hand from his and began clearing the table, hoping he wouldn't see her feelings in her eyes. "I hope so," she finally answered, trying to sound casual.

Edward watched her as she worked. He'd noticed her clothes the minute she'd opened the door, but he hadn't commented on them for fear she would change. The worn T-shirt clung to her breasts. Her cutoffs were short and tight, showing plenty of leg and emphasizing her cute fanny. "Maribeth?" He almost croaked her name.

Maribeth's stomach lurched at the husky sound of his voice. She turned off the water and dried her hands on a towel. It hit her suddenly how she was dressed, and she blushed. Hunger had preempted all thoughts of changing into more appropriate clothing. She turned around slowly and held her breath. "Yes?"

"Come here." It wasn't a request, it was a demand.

She moved slowly across the kitchen to where he was sitting. He opened his arms and she went willingly onto his lap. His thighs were hard beneath her hips. He tucked her head under his chin and held her for a moment. "I've missed you." She nodded in agreement.

He put his arms around her waist and locked his fingers together as though afraid she might move away. "I'm not going to pressure you into going to bed with me anymore. At least I'm going to *try* not to pressure you," he added, realizing how difficult it would be.

"Edward . . ."

"Shhh. Let me finish. I realize I've been acting like a fifteen-year-old who has just learned about sex." He squirmed in his chair, and the action drew Maribeth even closer to the area of his body that seemed to be giving him the most difficulty. "The only excuse I can offer is you excite me more than any woman I've ever met." He shook his head in frustration. "I've known a lot of women in my life, Maribeth, but none of them ever gave me the hard time you do or made sleeping at night impossible."

"I'm sorry. I don't mean to," she said honestly. But secretly she was pleased. It was a heady, exhilarating feeling knowing she had that much power over him.

He sighed. "I know you don't. But I'm prepared to back off now if that's what you want. I realize you need more time. And I'm sure Moss isn't making things easier—and neither am I with all the problems I'm having at the bank. But I want you to try to have enough faith in me to know I'm working as hard as I can to make it successful."

"I'm trying," she said truthfully. She stared at the calendar on the wall behind him, unable to make eye contact with him. "I suppose what you said yesterday was true," she confessed. "I've always let Moss make my decisions for me. I don't know when he started doing it; probably ever since kindergarten." She laughed. "He and I were quite a pair. He gave me advice and I tried to keep him out of fights. Maybe that's why I decided to go off to Atlanta. I needed to be my own person, do things my way for once. Moss says I've changed. Perhaps I have."

Edward gazed at her thoughtfully. "Well, you're certainly outspoken. I can't imagine anyone ever forcing you to do something against your will. I suppose every one of us has a bully in his life. My father was to me what Moss was to you. He used every argument he could think of to keep me from coming here. I was the genius of Wall Street, he told me, and I would be wasting my talents in a hick town like Laurel." He smiled and tucked a stray curl behind her ear. "Little did he know that this town would give me the substance I'd been missing all my life."

Maribeth relaxed against him as he talked, loving the warmth and strength of him. She buried her face against the hollow of his throat and inhaled his scent. She didn't ever want to leave his arms, preferring to remain there and feel his calm, even breathing. She knew in that instant she loved him. That knowledge jolted her to the soles of her feet.

She glanced up at him and wondered if he suspected. His gaze was tender and caring. She could only stare back at him and drink in the handsome features of his face. She wondered what her expression told him, because he lowered his mouth to hers and captured her lips in a warm kiss.

The kiss said it all. His lips moved over hers—tenderly at first, then hungrily, prodding her mouth open to receive his tongue. His hands were big and warm and slightly roughened as he cupped her cheeks, forcing her to remain perfectly still under the sensual onslaught of kisses. She could only moan her pleasure as his lips traced the path to one earlobe.

He slid his hands from her cheeks to her shoulders, pulling her closer, pressing her soft breasts against his chest. His lips moved over her face, raining kisses across her closed eyelids. She tasted so damn good, he couldn't get enough of her. His mouth moved almost frantically along the column of her throat before finding her earlobe. He nipped it with his teeth and delighted at making her squirm in his lap. She was made of wonderful textures, silk and satin, the same textures, he'd loved to feel in the dresses his mother wore when he was a child.

Maribeth's head swam as Edward's deft fingers tugged at the neck of her T-shirt, baring one shoulder and branding her flesh with his lips. His breath fanned warm across her skin, and goose pimples popped out on her flesh. When his hands cupped her breasts, it seemed only natural. She had been waiting for it.

Her head fell back as he leaned forward and sought her nipples with his lips. He took one between his teeth, T-shirt and all, and teased it until it hardened. The fabric rubbing against the quivering bud only heightened Maribeth's arousal, and she whimpered, feeling the heat surge to her thighs. Edward moved his lips to the other nipple, leaving the one he'd kissed quivering beneath the damp circle of her shirt. She could only lie against his shoulder and give in to the wonderful sensations. What was this power he had over her? she wondered. Edward had only to touch her with the lightness of a moth's wing to bring her to a heady state of arousal. She sighed blissfully, closing her eyes and letting herself delight in the nearness of him. Suddenly her eyes flew open, and she blinked at the calendar on the wall.

Edward sensed a change in her immediately. "What's wrong?"

"Today is Thursday."

"Yes, why?"

"I was supposed to be at the Community Club meeting about five minutes ago."

He tightened his grip on her, not willing to let her go just now. "You can miss it."

Her voice was apologetic. "I'm on one of the committees, and I have to give a report tonight. I only got the job last week because the lady who had it before me had to go into the hospital. Anyway, the Community Club is putting on a fair in nine days. I *have* to be there."

"Okay," he said. "I'll take you."

She pulled herself out of his lap. "You don't have to."

"Your car isn't running right, remember?"

"Oh, yeah, I forgot." She didn't have time to argue. "I appreciate it, Edward. Really I do." She hurried out of the room.

Maribeth was dressed in record time. When they arrived at the Community Club, she was relieved to see the meeting had not yet started, and people were mingling, sipping apple cider and munching on cookies that one of the members had provided. She froze when Moss walked through the door with lovely Jani-Sue Billings, who moved with the grace of a queen, her red hair flowing down her back in generous waves.

"Hello, Maribeth," Jani-Sue said, coming up to stand beside them. Moss followed. "Mr. Spears," she said, nodding politely to Edward and holding out her hand. "I'm Jani-Sue Billings. I believe you know my grandfather, Hector." She smiled. "He's told me all about you."

"He has?" Edward looked pleased.

"Have you met Moss Gentry?" she asked.

"We've had the pleasure," Moss muttered.

Maribeth stood in silence. Of all times for Jani-Sue to show up, she thought. Whenever the woman was around, Maribeth felt she had a three-inch wart on her nose.

"I understand you're from New York," Jani-Sue said. "We might know some of the same people. I worked there for several years."

"Jani-Sue is a model," Maribeth said to Edward, knowing anyone who laid eyes on her would guess as much.

Moss spoke up. "You two ought to get together sometime and discuss the city," he said, while Maribeth went into a slow burn. Moss's next statement was aimed at Jani-Sue. "I'm sure Mr. Spears misses the hustle and bustle of big-city life." He would have been blind not to see the daggers Maribeth was shooting his way. "I'm surprised he's lasted in Laurel as long as he has."

Jani-Sue smiled at Edward, showing a mouthful of beautiful white teeth. "Well, once you've lived here, it's hard to get the place out of your system. I hope you find it that way, too, Edward."

Maribeth wanted to applaud the woman. Behind her, Moss was a frowning giant. Obviously Jani-Sue had not accomplished what he'd hoped for. Jani-Sue glanced around the room. "I'd better go," she said. "I've got Grandpa's notes." She held up a worn notebook as proof.

"Is Hector here?" Edward asked. "I haven't seen him."

"Of course, he is," Janie-Sue said. "He's the president of the club. Has been for fifteen years now." She smiled at Maribeth and Edward. "I'll see you two later. Moss, are you sitting with me?" He nodded, a sour look on his face.

Hector Billings, wearing a faded blue cap and olive-green work pants, called the meeting to order and began discussing plans for the fair, which would pay for a playground the club hoped to build on a vacant lot that had been donated to them. "I'd like to hear from the committee heads," he said, hitching his pants up. "Who wants to go first?"

Sara Rawlings raised her hand. She was in charge of advertising. Behind her back people had laughingly said that since Sara was the town gossip, she shouldn't have any trouble getting word out about the fair. "The posters are ready to go up," she said, "and I've got several schoolboys already distributing the flyers."

Hector nodded. "Okay, who's in charge of the booths?"

Maribeth raised her hand and stood. "I am," she said. She gave Hector an apologetic smile. "I'm afraid I haven't had much time to work on it, but I promise to have everything under control by the time the fair opens." She glanced down at the small tablet she was holding. "Okay, I have all the volunteers I need for the craft booths. I also have people working the fishing booth, the ring toss, and the dart throw, but—" she looked up and grinned—"I don't have anybody for the kissing booth or the dunking booth. Any volunteers?"

The group chuckled. Finally one man spoke up. "I nominate Jani-Sue Billings for the kissing booth," he said, and his wife nudged him hard.

Maribeth glanced at Jani-Sue, who was considering the idea. She stood. "Okay, I'll do it," she said. "Under one condition." The group waited expectantly. "The cost of the kisses will be raised from one dollar to one fifty." There were groans from some of the men, but they finally agreed on the price.

"Thank you, Jani-Sue," Maribeth said, scribbling her name on the pad. "Now, who wants to volunteer for the dunking booth?" She wasn't surprised when nobody raised his hand. It wasn't a popular job. She looked at Hector and shrugged.

Hector put his hands on his hips. "Okay, now,

somebody has to do it," he said, "I'd do it myself if it weren't for my arthritis, but that cold water makes my joints stiff. How about you, O'Malley?" he said to Gus O'Malley, who owned O'Malley's Garage. "You did a good job last year."

"Yeah, and I almost caught pneumonia. Forget it, Hector. I done had my turn."

Moss Gentry raised his hand. "I nominate Edward Spears for the job," he said. "If he wants to become a member of this club, he should pull his weight like the rest of us."

Maribeth felt like pulling Moss's pocket knife out and cutting off his tongue. She glanced down at Edward.

Edward, who'd been considering it anyway, merely nodded. "I'll do it," he said, then grinned. "How bad can it be?"

Maribeth's lips twitched at the corners as she scribbled Edward's name on the list. She was already beginning to feel sorry for him. "How bad can it be?" he'd asked. Well, he was going to find out before long.

Six

All the booths had been set up, including the refreshment booths, and the air was filled with tempting smells of hot dogs, popcorn, and cotton candy. It was the first week of April, but the temperature was cooler than usual, and a nippy breeze had forced many people into their sweaters.

Maribeth had rented a shorty clown suit for the occasion and wondered if it had been a good idea after all.

"Why are you dressed like that?" Edward asked soon after his arrival. He was dressed in jeans and a long-sleeved pullover and carried his bathing suit and towel under one arm. With the dip in the temperature he was already beginning to think he'd made a mistake by volunteering for the dunking booth.

"Because I want to attract attention to our booth," Maribeth said, her heart skipping a beat as it usually did when he was around. They'd spent a lot of time together lately, not only at the bank, but at Edward's house, where he did the cooking. It was a joke between them that he was teaching Maribeth how to cook and that was why she needed to eat there every night. He'd been true to his promise about keeping his distance, though, and she had begun to worry that something was wrong with her. "Whoever takes in the most money tonight wins a prize," she continued. "It's a gigantic picnic basket filled with goodies." She smiled. "If we win, we can go on a picnic tomorrow."

He looked skeptical. "Don't get your hopes up. Jani-Sue already has a dozen men standing in line, and she hasn't even opened her booth yet."

"So I see," Maribeth muttered, glancing toward Jani-Sue's booth. "Perhaps we'd make more money selling ChapStick." She glanced back at him. "You'd better get dressed. Or should I say undressed?"

He grinned. "I love it when you talk dirty to me."

Maribeth watched him go, his wide shoulders and slender hips causing her to stare with feminine appreciation. She knew in her heart she loved him, yet couldn't bring herself to say the words out loud. But if he truly cared for her, he would have surely broken his promises about not pushing her into lovemaking. Instead, he seemed to avoid getting close to her.

Her thoughts were interrupted by the sudden appearance of Moss. "Pity it's not warmer tonight," he said, dipping one hand into the tank of water. "But then that would take the fun out of it, wouldn't it?" He winked at her. "I like your clown suit. Why don't you and me get together later and do a little clowning around? Get it? Clowning around?"

She gave him a bored look. "Drop dead, Moss."

"You've lost your sense of humor, Maribeth," he said in a wounded tone. "The only reason I bothered showing up tonight was to give you a bit of news. I hear lover boy has been checking on flights to New York."

"So? What if Edward *is* checking on flights? It's a free world."

"Just thought I'd let you know. Edward Spears doesn't belong here. Maybe he's finally come to realize it."

Maribeth was thankful when Moss left. She hadn't

wanted him to see how his news had shocked her. She knew Moss well enough to realize he wouldn't just make something up like that. He would find great pleasure delivering the news to her personally, once he knew, but he wouldn't tell her a lie.

When she spotted Edward in his bathing trunks, it took her breath away. She watched in fascination as he walked toward her. His bathing suit rode low on his hips, right beneath his navel, where black hair whorled around it in a most interesting way. His chest was wide and matted with thick black hair that ran down to his flat stomach. His legs were long and finely muscled. "Where should I put my clothes?" he asked, holding out his bundle.

"I'll take them," she mumbled, trying not to stare.

"I just want to know one thing," he said. "If we win, will you really go with me on a picnic tomorrow?"

Before or after you leave for New York, she wanted to ask. Instead, she merely nodded.

"Good. I'll try to remember that while I'm up there freezing to death." He grinned. "By the way, your fanny looks great in that outfit." As if to prove that point, he whacked her playfully on the behind before making his way to the tank.

A loudspeaker squealed in the background and someone put on a record, blasting carnival music everywhere. People began filing through the gates in numbers. Maribeth was going to have to worry about Edward later.

"Step right up, folks," she said, "and try your luck at dunking the banker. Better do it now," she jeered, "before he raises your interest rates."

One man stopped. "What do I have to do?"

"Pay me fifty cents, and you get three balls," she told him. He paid her and took the balls. On the third throw Edward plunged into the water. "Good shot!"

she said. "Anybody else?" She glanced at the crowd. Several others came up.

Two hours later Maribeth's voice had grown hoarse, but a crowd had gathered at the booth. While Edward frowned and shivered from his seat above the tank, she counted change and brought in customers, either through flirtation or outright intimidation. Jani-Sue, she noticed, had closed her booth early, despite the steady stream of customers.

When Maribeth had decided Edward should take a break, she sent for hot dogs and coffee and called him down. He flashed her an accusing look as he took the plastic cup from her. "Do you have to be so good at this?" he muttered crossly. His towel was draped across his shoulders but didn't prevent him from getting cold. "Now I know why nobody else wanted this job. Next year, I'm going to pay Moss back by nominating him for it."

Next year? she wondered. "We'll be able to close soon," she said. "Jani-Sue closed her booth an hour ago."

Edward took a sip of his coffee. "I'm sure she was as tired of her job as I am mine."

Thirty minutes later Maribeth was still handing out balls. She looked up and found Gertrude Givens standing in line. "I'd like to buy twenty dollars worth of balls," the woman said.

"Twenty dollars?" Maribeth said in disbelief. "But they don't cost that much."

"I know that," Gertrude said in the same snippety tone she'd used in Edward's office the day they'd had the confrontation over loan-application forms. "But I'm not good at hitting targets. I figure for twenty dollars I should be able to throw till I knock him in. Even if it takes all night."

With a barely suppressed smile Maribeth handed her the balls, hoping for Edward's sake, it wouldn't take all night. Gertrude had to throw the ball fifteen times before she slammed Edward into the water, all the while glaring at him as if he were a housefly about to get swatted. She dusted her hands and smiled at Maribeth. "It was worth every penny," she said, very pleased with herself. Then she strutted off, her old hat lopsided on her head.

Maribeth was still laughing when Edward climbed down from the tank. "I fail to see the humor in it," he said. "That woman was out for blood." He gathered up his dry clothes. "I refuse to go back up there. I have too many enemies in this town." He headed off in the direction of the men's restroom.

Maribeth went about the business of closing down the booth. She opened the cashbox and began counting the money they had made and was surprised to see they'd done so well. Maybe she and Edward should go into the dunking business, she thought. She laughed out loud at the thought and glanced up just in time to see him come out of the men's room. From out of nowhere Jani-Sue appeared, still wearing the midnight-blue evening gown she'd worn for the kissing booth. Maribeth watched them converse briefly. What she saw next made her heart sink. Edward followed Jani-Sue into the parking lot.

How long Maribeth stood there staring at the throng of cars where they had disappeared, she didn't know. She suddenly realized that someone was speaking to her and looked up to find Dan and Carol.

"Where'd Slick run off to?" Dan asked. "I was going to try my luck at dunking him in that tank of water."

Maribeth put a rubber band around the bills. "He and Jani-Sue disappeared into the parking lot about ten minutes ago.

Dan's mouth dropped open. "For what?" Carol nudged him hard with her elbow.

"How should I know?" Maribeth was trying not to let

her mind run wild with thoughts of what might be going on.

"Come have a cup of coffee with us," Carol said.

"Yeah," Dan agreed. "Stop clowning around and come with us."

"Do you mind, Dan?" Maribeth said. "I've had it up to here with clown jokes." She relented. "Okay. But first I have to drop this money off."

"Where?" Dan asked.

"To Hector. He's running the cotton candy machine."

When they got to the refreshment booth, there was no sign of Hector. The cotton candy stand had closed down at least half an hour ago, they were told. Maribeth finally located the treasurer of the Community Club and passed the money to her, then joined Dan and Carol for coffee at one of the small tables near the refreshment booth.

They had only been seated about ten minutes when they saw Edward and Jani-Sue stumble out of the parking lot. They were laughing, and when they spotted the three of them sitting at the table, they hurried toward them. Edward was staggering and Jani-Sue kept tripping over her long dress.

"I hate to say this, but those two look drunk," Dan said.

"Well, hellooo" Jani-Sue called out in a singsong voice. "We've been looking everywhere for you, Maribeth."

"Oh? I didn't go anywhere," she said stiffly.

Edward pulled out a chair and slumped into it, a silly lopsided grin on his face. "How much money did we make?" he asked, slurring his words badly.

Maribeth caught the strong smell of alcohol and frowned. "Did you just rob a liquor store?"

Edward threw his head back and laughed. "D'you hear that?" he asked Dan, slapping him on the knee. "She asked me—"

Dan was grinning. "Yeah, I heard. Pretty funny stuff, huh?"

Jani-Sue put her hands on the back of a chair to steady herself. "I hope you won't be mad at Edward," she said to Maribeth. "Grandpa asked me to fetch him so he could have a taste of his home brew." She glanced doubtfully at Edward, who seemed to be in a semistupor at the moment. "I don't think Edward is accustomed to moonshine."

Dan nodded. "They probably don't serve a lot of it in New York."

Maribeth saw the glazed look in Edward's eyes. She had heard about Hector's brew and what it did to people. She stood abruptly. "I'm taking you home, Edward. You're in no condition to drive."

Edward tried to stand. It took several attempts. He had to grab hold of the table for support. "Thas . . . not . . . necess . . . necess . . . uh . . ."

"Necessary," Dan supplied for him.

"You're riding home with me," Maribeth repeated in an authoritative voice, and grabbed his arm. She said her good-byes to the others and headed toward the parking lot. It took her fifteen minutes to get Edward to the car.

"Can you b'lieve it?" Edward said for the umpteenth time. "Hector Billings invited me to his pickup for some homemade whiskey." He stopped and grabbed her by the shoulders. "D'ja hear that?" he insisted in a loud voice.

"Yes, Edward. I heard you the first three times you told me." She led him around to the passenger's side of the car and helped him in.

It was going to be a long ride, she thought. She climbed in on the other side of the car and held her breath as she turned the key in the ignition. Much to her surprise the motor roared to life.

They made the drive to Edward's house in silence,

and Maribeth glared at him whenever it looked as though he was going to fall asleep.

"Stay where you are," she said as she pulled into his driveway. "I'll help you out of the car."

He frowned. "You think I'm drunk, but I'm not," he said matter-of-factly. "I happen to be in complete control of my . . . uh, my faculties." He opened his door and stepped out of the car. He tripped on the edge of the driveway and fell face-first on the grass.

Maribeth gave a small squeal and hurried out of the car and around to the other side. Edward was sprawled across the front lawn. "Are you okay?" she asked, getting down on her hands and knees beside him.

He raised his head with some effort. "I'm okay," he mumbled, "but I think I put a dent in my lawn."

"Here, let me help you up," she said, trying to pull him to his feet. She wrapped one of his arms around her shoulder. "Can you walk?"

"Of course, I can walk. I have legs, don't I?" He stopped briefly and glanced down as if to make sure they were still there. He continued to hold on to her as they made their way up the front walk. He took a deep breath, trying to clear his head. Her perfume was everywhere. "You smell good," he said, turning and putting his face in her hair. "I've always loved the way you smell."

Maribeth's pulse quickened in response. "I wish I could say the same about you," she said, her mood still sour. "You smell like one hundred fifty proof." Once she got him to the door, she let go. "Where are your keys?"

Edward weaved as he reached into his pocket for them. He tried several times to slip the key into the lock but failed. "Darn keyhole keeps moving on me," he muttered, trying once more.

Maribeth sighed. "Give them to me," she said, taking

them from him. She easily slipped the key into the lock.

"How'd you do that?"

She opened the door and helped him inside. "Where's the light switch?"

"Uh, let me think." He was silent for a minute as Maribeth tried to feel for the light switch in the darkness. All at once she felt his arms snake around her waist.

"What do you think you're doing?" she shrieked in surprise.

"I like it dark," he said, pulling her close. "The light from the moon is shining on your hair." He nuzzled his face in her hair. "I luff your hair, you know that?"

"All I know is, you're very drunk," she said, struggling.

"I'm drunk on luff," he said, working his way to her earlobe.

"Oh, give me a break," she said. Nevertheless, chills were parading up her spine.

His hands were everywhere. "I know I promised not to touch you and all that, but uh, well—"

She sighed. "Never mind. I need to get you to bed," she said, once again putting his arm over his shoulder. "Which way's the bedroom?"

"This way," he said, and led her up the stairs.

Once they reached the bedroom, Maribeth switched on the light.

"Oh, Lord," Edward said, covering his eyes with one hand. "Did you have to do that?"

"Sit on the bed so I can get your boots off," she said.

Edward did as he was told. "Now what?" he asked, after she'd removed both boots.

"What do you usually sleep in?"

"Nothing."

"Oh well, it looks like you're going to sleep in your clothes tonight."

"Are you staying? Please say yes. I wish you could

just stay for one night," he said, as she helped him lie back on the bed. "Do you know what I really wish?"

He looked so vulnerable at the moment, Maribeth felt her heart soften. "What do you wish, Edward?" she asked tenderly.

"I wish I hadn't fallen on the lawn. I think I broke my nose. Does it look broken to you?"

"No," she said. Serves him right, though, she thought.

He closed his eyes and she was about to leave when he spoke again. "Do you know what I luff most about you?" he said.

"What?" She held her breath.

"You. I luff you, Maribeth."

She felt her heart slam into her throat. "I love you, too, Edward," she said breathlessly, and asked, "so why are you checking on flights to New York?" There was no answer. He'd already begun to snore.

It was almost eleven o'clock the following morning when Maribeth heard someone knock at her door. She hurried to the door, opened it, and was not surprised to find Edward on the other side. He looked frantic.

"Have you seen my car?"

It took every ounce of willpower to keep from smiling. "Your car?" she said innocently, taking in the bloodshot eyes with smug satisfaction. Served him right for passing out before she could question him about New York. Now she was determined not to mention it. Let him tell her himself.

"Yes, I lost it. At least I think I did. I looked in the driveway this morning, and it was gone."

"Oh, Edward," she said, feeling the corners of her mouth twitch. "Your car is at the fairgrounds where you left it. You were in no condition to drive, so I drove you home."

He gave a sigh of relief. "Well, that's good news," he said.

She couldn't help but laugh. "Come on in and let me pour you a cup of coffee."

"I could use a couple of aspirin as well," he said, sitting down at the kitchen table.

Maribeth left the room and returned a minute later with a bottle of aspirin. She set it on the table and went to the sink to fill a glass with water. "You don't look well," she said, studying his pale face.

"Believe me, I feel worse than I look," he said. "On top of having what is probably the worst hangover in history, I think I'm getting a cold from spending the night immersed in ice water." As if on cue, he sneezed loudly.

Feeling a bit more sympathetic, Maribeth poured him a cup of coffee and carried it to him. "In a little while you'll be good as new," she said encouragingly.

"I doubt I'll ever be back to normal after drinking Hector's so-called brew."

"Good grief, Edward. Have you any idea what that stuff can do to a person? It could kill you."

"I *had* to drink it," he said, "especially since Hector had all his friends there. Think how it would have looked if I had refused to drink with them." He attempted to smile. "I appreciate you driving me home."

"We're just lucky my car has been running the past couple of days. One of my neighbors is letting me use his battery charger until I buy a new battery." She noticed Edward's hair was a bit disheveled. He looked quite sexy like that.

"Did you walk here?" she asked.

"No, I made the mistake of calling a cab."

She laughed. "We only have one cab in Laurel."

"So I learned. I had to wait an hour." Someone knocked on the kitchen door and Maribeth glanced up.

"Wonder who that could be?" She peeked through the curtain. "It's Hector."

"Don't tell him I'm hung over," Edward said, hiding the aspirin bottle.

Maribeth threw open the door. "I don't believe it!" she squealed in delight, finding Hector holding a large picnic basket. "Did we win?" She held the door open so he could pass through.

"You sure did." He grinned and set the basket on the kitchen table. "I oughta tell you, Jani-Sue is spitting mad. Said she had to kiss all those ugly farmers for nothing. I told her it was her fault for closing down so early." He glanced at Edward. "How you feeling this morning?"

"Great!" Edward said, as though he couldn't be better. "Just great."

"There's enough food here for an army," Maribeth said, looking at the basket.

Hector smiled and nodded. "Well, that twenty-dollar bill clinched it. I figured if you could convince some fool to pay twenty dollars to dunk this man, you deserved it. Well, got to run. Jani-Sue is waiting in the truck."

"You know who we have to thank for this, don't you?" Maribeth said to Edward as soon as Hector was gone. "That twenty-dollar bill belonged to Gertrude Givens."

"Well, forgive me if I don't share your gratitude," he said wryly, then smiled at her enthusiasm. "Do you think we can eat all that?"

"You don't really feel like going on a picnic, do you?"

He stood and smiled. "I just started feeling one hundred percent better, knowing I get to spend the day with you. Where should we go?"

"I know a great place. We can take my car."

"Do you think it'll start?"

"I think so. I feel lucky today."

He gave her a big smile. "So do I."

• • •

An hour later they climbed out of Maribeth's car and followed a narrow path through a patch of woods that, she claimed, held the perfect picnic spot. The sun was warm on her face as she led the way through the thick trees. Edward was right behind her, carrying the large picnic basket. "How much farther is this picnic spot, Yogi?" he asked, puffing from the heavy load.

She giggled. "Hang in there, Boo Boo, it's not far." She heard the sound of running water and knew they were close. All at once the dense brush opened into a clearing where a large pool was shimmering in the sun. A miniature waterfall gushed forth on the other side and sprayed into the pool. "Well, what do you think?" she asked, seeing the stunned look on Edward's face.

"Wow! How'd you ever find this place?"

"I use to roam these woods as a kid. Did I ever mention I was a tomboy?"

"I think I just assumed it the first time I saw you handle a gun."

"Come on," she said. "There's a huge flat rock on top we can sit on." She stopped at the edge of the water. "We're going to have to walk on these smaller rocks to get to the big boulder. Be careful, they're slippery."

Edward followed her across the rocks that led to the boulder. When they reached the boulder, Maribeth spread out the quilt she'd been carrying and sat down. Edward joined her, still amazed by the sight. It was beautiful. He took a deep breath. The air was fresh and crisp, but much warmer. His head had stopped hurting. "Do you mind if I take off my shirt?" he asked.

Maribeth, who'd been admiring the scenery as well, glanced at him in surprise. "Uh, go ahead," she said, trying to sound casual. It was going to be an impossible afternoon, she told herself.

Edward unbuttoned his shirt and shrugged it off, feeling her eyes on him. The thought that she might find him attractive appealed to him. He was certainly attracted to her.

"Shall we see what's in the basket?" Maribeth said, trying not to stare at his broad chest. She already knew how devastatingly sexy he was, and being so close and alone with him made it hard to think. She lifted the old-fashioned red-and-white checkered cloth.

"What's in there?" Edward asked, noticing how quiet she'd become.

"Oh, all kinds of goodies," she said. She pulled out dark onion rolls, egg rolls, and rye. Beneath that lay different kinds of meats and cheeses. She laughed. "It's obvious Hector didn't buy this basket around here," she said, "or we would have had fried chicken and buttermilk biscuits. Look, we even have plates and glasses and silverware and napkins. And a bottle of wine." She smiled at Edward. "Aren't you glad you volunteered for the dunking booth now?"

"I didn't volunteer. Moss nominated me, remember? What kind of wine is it?" He took the bottle from her and glanced at the label. "Not bad."

"I'm afraid I'm not much on wine," she confessed, "but I do know what this is for." She held up a corkscrew. She watched Edward peel the wrapper away, puncture the cork, and twist the corkscrew. The muscles in his arms rippled as his long fingers turned the corkscrew with little effort. Her gaze slid up his arms to his shoulders, then dropped to his chest. His chest hair glistened in the sunlight. She glanced away when he looked up suddenly and caught her staring. "Do you . . . uh, feel like having any wine?" she asked, trying to keep her mind off his body. "I mean, with your headache and all?"

He shrugged and pulled out the cork with a popping sound. "We ought to have a celebration toast." He took one of the glasses and poured it half full before handing it to her, then poured less for himself. He set the bottle down and held up his glass for a toast. "What should we drink to?"

Maribeth thought for a minute. "Gertrude Givens?"

He frowned. "Surely we can think of something better than that." He dropped the frown. "To us," he said, holding his glass up and touching hers. "May all our differences fall to the side and our relationship grow in love." He grinned. "How was that?"

It took Maribeth a few seconds to find her tongue. "Heavens. When you make a toast, you don't mess around." She took a tentative sip as she watched him drain his glass. "I can't really drink much," she said, licking a drop of the wine from the corner of her lips. She was still very much affected by his little speech. "Wine goes straight to my head."

Edward hadn't missed the pink tongue darting out of the corner of her mouth. "What happens after it goes to your head?"

"I get giggly. And lovable."

He reached for the bottle. "Have some more."

She laughed and held her glass out of reach. "I'm not finished with what I have."

"Just kidding. When you decide to become lovable with me, I don't want you to be intoxicated." His eyes were on her lips as he spoke. "I want all your pretty little senses intact when I make love to you."

"Edward!" She blushed. "I think we'd better eat something," she said, busying herself with the food preparations. Anything to get their conversation onto another subject. Something safe. "What do you want?" she asked, wishing her voice didn't quaver so.

"I think we both know the answer to that."

Nothing was safe with this man. "To eat," she said, thoroughly frustrated.

"I'll have ham and cheese on rye. In there a knife in there?"

"Uh-huh." It took several minutes to unwrap the

ham and slice it into edible pieces. Making the sandwiches was even more difficult, and Edward watched her every move. When she finally handed him his sandwich, she was thankful he had something to concentrate on other than her. After they had eaten, Edward rolled his shirt up into a makeshift pillow, tucked it beneath his head and lay back. He watched Maribeth repack the basket. She looked pensive.

"What are you thinking?" he asked.

She looked up in surprise. He never missed a thing. "Oh, I was just thinking about my parents. I usually visit them on Sunday."

"Feeling guilty?"

She shrugged. "A little."

"Come here," he said, holding one arm out for her.

She hesitated. His open arms represented both comfort and danger. But she was already hopelessly in love with him, wasn't she? She was powerless with him and knew it. She lay down beside him, cushioning her head in the crook of his arm. His flesh was warm against her cheek. His chest hair reminded her of the Spanish moss that hung from the limbs of the live oaks, yet she knew his hair would feel like coarse silk between her fingers. His flat stomach was etched with muscles and feathered lightly with the same dark hair. She ached to touch him, to experience each texture she saw there. As if reading her thought, Edward took her hand and placed it on her chest. Maribeth felt her heart leap into her throat. She pulled back slightly, but his large hand on hers stopped her.

"Don't be afraid to touch me," he said, caressing her hand. "Touching is good for the spirit. Didn't you know that?"

Her stomach fluttered at the velvet-edged tone, but she didn't withdraw her hand. Even though the heat of his flesh seemed to burn straight through her palm, she remained perfectly still. It was a wonderful moment for her, yet awkward. "Tell me about your family," she blurted out, trying to think of something to say.

He chuckled softly when he heard the strain in her voice. He *wanted* her to be comfortable touching him. "I've already told you some things about them," he said, "the other night at my place." The night he had ached so desperately to make love to her in the firelight. "My father is a banker like me, and my mother involves herself with various charities she believes in. Does that answer your question?"

"Are they rich?" She imagined they'd have to be rich to live in New York.

He smiled. What Maribeth lacked in tact she made up for her in her sweetness. "Rich, no. But they live comfortably."

"Why weren't they close to your grandfather?"

"Mainly because my father and my grandfather were so different. They each had different ideas on how a bank should be run."

"Which one of them do you think you're most like?" she asked, gazing up at his tanned face. She relaxed against him, enjoying the clean, masculine scent of his flesh. The moment seemed intimate, yet completely natural.

"I hope I'm a little of both," he said. He stroked her hair as he talked, twirling the thick strands around his fingers in ways he'd only dreamed of doing.

"What were you like as a boy?" she asked.

"I suppose I was like most boys, in and out of mischief. We lived in a high-rise building, very nice, very chic, but no backyard to play in. I think that's what I missed most about my childhood. Everything in New York is tight and compact, not like the wide-open space out here. We had a housekeeper named Hildegarde, still do as a matter of fact, a big German woman who taught me how to make up a bed Army-regulation style.

If my bed wasn't just so, she'd jerk the covers off and make me start over."

"She doesn't sound like she was very pleasant," Maribeth said.

"I never really knew if Hildegarde liked me until one day I came home with a puppy. He was a stray; there were no tags. The only thing I ever wanted in my whole life was my own dog." He laughed as he remembered. "Somehow I managed to slip the dog past the doorman and up to our apartment without being caught. Naturally Hildegarde found out."

"And blew the whistle on you?"

"No. As a matter of fact, she helped me hide the pup. We kept food in my closet and papers on the floor for him to use. But Hildegarde warned me we wouldn't be able to keep him hidden for long." He laughed. "We made it three whole days before my parents found out."

"What happened?"

"My father took him to the animal shelter and that was that."

"It must've hurt."

"I cried for a week. My parents tried to make me understand, we just couldn't have a pet in the apartment. They even took me to Coney Island the following weekend to make up for it. I still want a dog, though, a golden retriever, I think."

"What's stopping you?" She held her breath for an answer.

"I don't know. I'm just not sure . . . of some things."

Her heart sank. "So Hildegarde is still with your parents?"

"Oh, yes." She runs the place, and they do as they're told.

Maribeth laughed. "I'd like to meet her."

"You'd like her. She's just . . . Hildegarde," he said, unable to think of a word to describe her.

Maribeth closed her eyes, content to lie in his arms while he talked, telling her pieces of his life. His soothing voice rocked her like no melody could. A gentle breeze whispered across the rock where they lay and played with the curls at her cheek. The sound of water splashing gently into the pool below made her smile. All was right with the world today, she thought, and she was in the arms of the man she loved. Tomorrow might bring fears and uncertainly, but today was hers. Beside her Edward closed his eyes as well.

Seven

They awoke sometime later to the first drops of rain.
The sun had slipped behind a cloud, making the day
gloomy. Maribeth blinked her eyes for a moment until
she remembered where she was.

"We'd better get this stuff picked up," Edward said,
still groggy from sleep. He'd been dreaming that Maribeth
had awakened and begun undressing him right on the
rock. They had made love; wild, passionate love. And
she had been soft and beautiful beneath him. It made
his insides ache just to think about it.

Within minutes the rain was pelting against them,
icy cold on their skin. Edward threw on his shirt as
they grabbed their belongings and scrambled across
the stepping stones toward dry land. The trees offered
some protection, but still they got soaked. Edward began to sneeze.

The rain had slackened by the time they reached
Maribeth's car. Nevertheless, they were drenched and
weak with laughter. Maribeth's hair was plastered to
her scalp, as was her blouse to her breasts. Edward
fixed his gaze on the two enticing mounds. His hair
was wet as well. His shirt hung open and tiny rivulets

of water trickled down his chest and stomach. As they continued to stare at each other, the laughter died in their throats. Edward put down the basket and stepped closer.

Maribeth stood perfectly still as he slipped his hands on either side of her neck, lifting her damp hair. His eyes met hers, and the look in them took her breath away. He leaned forward and pressed warm lips beneath one earlobe. Then, slowly, very slowly, he kissed his way to the same pulse point on the other side, then back to the hollow of her throat. She dropped the quilt and grasped his shoulders for support, closing her eyes, letting her head fall back. He slipped his arms around her waist and pulled her close. He chuckled softly as a fat raindrop slid unobtrusively from her forehead down the length of her nose. He caught it with the tip of his tongue before pressing his lips to hers.

When Edward broke the kiss, Maribeth pressed her lips against his throat, dropping her arms from his shoulders to his waist, inside his wet shirt. His flesh was hot. Without thinking about her next move, she buried her face against his chest and inhaled his musky scent as she had yearned to do so often. The curls on his chest caressed her cheek like coarse silk. That, combined with the very masculine scent, worked like an aphrodisiac on her senses. She nuzzled the curls, sliding her hands from his waist and pressing her palms against his chest. His muscles flexed in response to her touch. His nubby brown nipples were erect, no doubt from the cool rain, and she touched one with her fingertip.

Maribeth looked into his eyes and saw her own desire mirrored there. She was moving to dangerous ground and she knew it, could see it in his compelling stare. But she could no more resist her next move than she could resist taking her next breath. Very slowly she lowered her mouth to his nipple and fastened it there, letting her warm tongue swirl around it, gaining as much pleasure from the experience as he. She felt him shiver. Then, much to her surprise, he sneezed. Again and again.

"Maribeth," he croaked. "I know I'm going to hate myself in the morning, but I think it's only fair to warn you, I'm getting a cold." He sighed. "And I'd hate to give it to you."

It took a minute for his words to sink in, then she raised her hand to his forehead. He was burning up! She had obviously mistaken his fever for desire. A hot blush spread across her face. "Oh, Edward, I'm so sorry," she said, moving quickly now. She opened the trunk to her car and tossed the quilt in. "I need to get you home."

He deposited the picnic basket next to the quilt. "I'd like to pick up my car first, if you don't mind dropping me by the fairgrounds."

"Are you sure you feel like driving?"

He nodded. "I'll be okay. It's only a cold." He shivered again. "I just want to get into some dry clothes." He saw the way she looked at him, her eyes soft and full of concern, and he knew he wouldn't have to wait until morning to hate himself for putting a stop to what had looked promising. He'd never seen her so loving and he was certain now there was a very passionate side to Maribeth Bradford. Of all times to feel rotten! But he wanted their first time together to be perfect. Heaven knew, she had enough doubts already.

"Here, let me help you into the car," she offered. "I'll drive."

He chuckled, despite the fact his headache had returned. "Maribeth, I'm not lame." He climbed into the car.

She joined him in the front seat. "I can call Doc Henderson if you like," she offered. "He makes house calls, you know."

"I don't need a doctor. I need a nice warm bed."

Maribeth drove to the fairgrounds as fast as she could. Edward's scowling face didn't prompt conversation. He obviously felt rotten.

"Are you sure you want to drive?" she asked when they reached his car.

"I'm okay," he mumbled. "I'll pick you up in the morning, and we'll look for you a new battery at lunchtime."

"You don't have to do that. I'm perfectly capable—"

"Don't argue," he said, climbing out of the car. "I'll pick you up at eight-thirty. Try to be ready." He closed the door.

Maribeth watched his retreating back. The old grump. Some men turned into big babies when they were sick, others were as grouchy as bears. Edward was both. A twinge of pity tugged her heart. What he needed was someone to take care of him; someone to make sure he stayed warm and took his medicine and spooned soup into him. She grinned. He needed her!

Maribeth rang Edward's doorbell two hours later. It had taken her that long to run home, shower and change, and go by the grocery store. She rang the bell again and shifted the grocery sack to her other arm.

Edward opened the door wearing his bathrobe. He blinked his sleep-filled eyes. "What are you doing here?"

She slipped through the opening of the door. "I'm here to take care of you," she said, heading straight for the kitchen. "Now you go back to bed and I'll make you something to eat."

He followed her. "I'm not hungry."

"You will be once you see all the goodies I've brought." She glanced at him and almost dropped her sack. His bathrobe hung open to the waist, exposing a large amount of chest. His thighs and legs were breathtakingly sexy beneath the short hem. "Go on," she insisted. "I'll be in shortly with a tray."

Edward raked his hand through his hair and shook his head. Arguing with her was useless. He padded barefoot out of the kitchen toward the bedroom.

Fifteen minutes later Maribeth knocked on Edward's bedroom door, carrying a tray laden with food. She found him in bed beneath the covers, propped on two pillows, watching television. His robe was draped over a chair, leaving him, once again, bare-chested. She swallowed. "You're supposed to be sleeping," she said in an authoritative voice.

"I was sleeping until you rang the doorbell," he said simply.

She set the tray carefully on his lap. Edward raised both brows when he saw the food. Besides soup and crackers, there was fresh fruit—honeydew melon and strawberries—and various cheeses. "You shouldn't have gone to so much trouble."

She shrugged. "No trouble." She glanced around the bedroom. The mahogany four-poster bed had no doubt belonged to his grandparents, as had the embroidered coverlet. A pair of Queen Anne chairs and a mahogany highboy and matching dresser was beautiful and elegant, slightly formal without being austere. Maribeth took one of the chairs.

"Aren't you having anything?" Edward asked.

"I had a couple of crackers with cheese earlier," she said.

He began to eat. "I'm real proud of you," he said. "You managed to cook an entire can of soup without burning it."

"Very funny."

"You're going to make somebody a wonderful wife. I believe the Campbell's Soup Company offers more than three dozen varieties."

"You're obviously feeling better," she said dully.

While he was eating she watched part of the program

he'd turned on. When he was finished, she took the tray and carried it back into the kitchen. "I'd better be going now," she said.

"Don't go yet," he said, not wanting her to leave.

"I have to."

"Then would you bring me a wet cloth before you go? I'm feeling a bit . . . uh . . . dizzy."

"You are?" she asked, noticing his voice had become weaker. "Why didn't you say something sooner?"

"I didn't want to bother you," he said, lying back on the pillow. He sighed heavily as though the mere effort of moving had cost him all his energy. "Just give me the cloth and you can leave."

"I'm not about to leave you if you're that sick," she said. "Where do you keep the washcloths?"

"Hall closet."

She hurried out of the room and returned a moment later with the damp cloth. She placed it gently on his forehead and tucked the covers around him as some maternal instinct took over. "Tell me how you feel," she said, stroking his forehead above the cloth, just below his hairline.

If only she knew, he thought. She would probably pull out one of her pistols if he told her how badly he wanted her right now. The nap and food and the little intimate things she had done for him to make him feel better had left him craving for her in a way that hurt. "The, uh, room is spinning a little," he said, feeling a bit guilty over the concerned look in her eyes. "Everything is blurred. I can barely see your face."

She moved closer, her brows drawn together in a worried frown. Perhaps she should call the doctor after all. "I'm here," she whispered reassuringly.

He caught the faint scent of honeysuckle. "Maybe you should come closer."

Maribeth caught the husky sound of his voice and frowned. He didn't sound sick. She studied him for a moment. His color was fine. And he didn't feel as hot as he had earlier. She pursed her lips. Perhaps he wasn't as sick as he wanted her to think he was. She leaned closer until her lips were almost touching his. She slipped one hand around his neck. "Oh, Edward," she whispered seductively. "I'll come as close as you like. I had no idea you were so . . . uh, sick."

Edward peered out at her from beneath partially closed eyes and saw the anxious look on her face. She had swallowed it. He felt her lips move to his forehead tenderly and almost sighed his contentment.

"Tell me what I can do to make you feel better," she said in a husky purr.

"Lie down beside me and hold me," he said weakly, "until the room stops spinning."

Without further prompting, Maribeth curled up beside him on the bed. He put his arm around her and placed her head in the crook of his shoulder. "Is that better?" she asked.

"Put your hand on my stomach and rub it gently," he said. He lifted the cover slightly to accommodate her.

Maribeth glanced up at him and saw the smile lurking in his eyes. "You say, you want me to rub your stomach?" she repeated, raising up on one elbow. "Well, forgive me, but I don't think it's your stomach giving you the most trouble; I think it's something else." She promptly removed the cold cloth from his forehead, slipped it beneath the covers, and dropped it onto his lap, blushing slightly at the sight of his white underwear. Edward jumped and muttered a curse. "You've got a fever, buddy," she said, "but not from your cold." She heard his muttered threat and tried to scramble from the bed. He grabbed her and pinned her down beneath him.

"You're going to pay for that," he said, grinning.

"Oh?" Her heart hammered wildly in her chest. She couldn't move beneath the weight of his chest. She didn't want to.

"I have a confession to make," he said. "I'm not really dizzy. I made it up just to get you into bed with me."

She didn't crack a smile. "I know."

He raised both brows in surprise. "You do?" When she nodded, he merely stared at her in silence. For weeks she had shied away from him, and now she was lying beneath him as though it were the most natural thing in the world. He looked deeply into her eyes and found them soft and full of emotion. He lowered his mouth to hers.

Maribeth felt her insides turn to mush. His mouth was warm and tasted of strawberries. He skillfully prodded her lips open and his tongue slipped past her teeth in a gentle exploration of her mouth. She snaked her arms around his neck, wanting to pull him even closer, despite the fact his body was already crushing wonderfully into hers. She slid her hands down his shoulders, delighting at the warm feel of his flesh, the hard muscles. She ran her hand lightly across his broad back, stopping at the elastic band of his underwear.

The lining of her mouth was like satin, Edward decided, and sweeter than honey. He broke the kiss and repositioned himself so she wasn't bearing the full brunt of his weight. He smiled and reached behind her head and opened the gold clasp that held back her thick hair. After tossing it aside, he combed his fingers through her hair until it fanned out across the pillow. But once he had it perfectly arranged, he grinned and mussed it. It looked like spun gold and felt like silk. He slid it through his fingers again and saw the curious look she gave him. He laughed self-consciously. "I've been wanting to play with your hair since I met you," he confessed, toying with a fat curl at her cheek. "Promise me you'll never have it cut."

She didn't have a chance to respond. His mouth took hers, this time hungrily. The kiss deepened. Edward's tongue played a delightful game of hide-and-seek with her own. The smell and taste of him made her giddy. He moved his lips to the base of her throat, and she grasped his shoulders once more, her uneven breathing competing with his. She closed her eyes as he pressed his body against hers intimately, letting her know of his desire. The warmth between her thighs turned hot. She arched her hips in response.

Edward's hands moved to the buttons on her blouse, working frantically to get them open while his lips sipped hers like fine wine. When he had managed to get her blouse and bra off, he merely stared at her in open adoration. Then without a word he lowered his lips to her breasts.

Maribeth sucked in her breath sharply as she felt the shock of warm lips covering the nipple of one breast. His tongue swirled around the dusky areola again and again until she began to breathe in tiny gulps. He nipped it gently with his teeth, then soothed it with a moist tongue.

His hand found its way to the fastening of her slacks.

Maribeth moaned, part pleasure, part restlessness, as his hands worked to remove her slacks. She raised herself slightly as he pushed them past her waist and hips to her knees, then she impatiently kicked them off. His hand returned to her thigh, warm and broad and wonderfully bold. He caressed her, and the heat of his flesh seemed to burn straight through the nylon panties. His lips never stopped, even as he busied his hands at the base of thighs, caressing, teasing, but never slipping inside the elastic band of her panties. Maribeth wanted to scream and tear them off and have him touch her flesh. Skin on skin. She could no longer think; she was a mass of sensations. She wanted him as she had never wanted a man in her life. She whispered his name in a plea as she arched her hips once more and buried her face in his neck.

Edward moved over her, thrilled with her passionate response. She was made for loving. He wanted their first time to be perfect, something she could burn into her memory forever, something that would wipe away her doubts and fears for the rest of her life. He removed her panties as she gazed up at him with desire. "You're beautiful," he said, his voice unsteady.

His lips reclaimed hers while his hand and fingers acquainted themselves with her flesh. Gently but thoroughly he explored the delicate area between her thighs, marveling at the satin texture. He located the very nucleus of her desire and brought her to full arousal, loving her twice as much when she responded with a honeyed warmth. Lord, how he wanted her!

He moved away just long enough to peel off his underwear. Maribeth's eyes roamed over his body freely, drinking in the sight she had only imagined in her dreams. Her dreams were nothing compared to the flesh-and-blood image before her. She held her arms out to receive him, knowing she loved him with all her heart.

His lips devoured hers as he probed cautiously between her thighs. But when he tried to enter, something stopped him. His eyes flew open. "Maribeth?"

"Don't stop!" she cried, her eyes pleading with him. "Now that we've come this far."

He was lost. He cursed himself mentally as he entered her slowly, tentatively, but firmly, pressing deeply into her satiny warmth, all the while scrutinizing her face for any sign of pain or displeasure. There was none. She sighed with extreme pleasure and pulled him closer. When he began to move against her, his thrusts were guarded. Nothing in his experience had prepared him for this, nor had it prepared him for what it was like making love to a woman he loved more than himself, more than life.

Maribeth rolled her head from side to side, her thoughts spinning. Each gentle thrust of Edward's body sent her further into oblivion. His hard body in hers was like the missing puzzle-piece in her universe. His lips and teeth toyed with an earlobe and sent shivers of delight up the back of her neck. He kissed and suckled at her breasts until she thought she would scream. The fire between her legs had grown out of control.

Edward stopped moving. She held him so tightly, so wonderfully. He was losing his mind. He began to move again, slowly, but every time he felt her muscles contract around him, he paid hell trying not to lose himself to the rapture he knew was but a breath away.

For Maribeth it was too late. She moved against him, urging him on even though he seemed to be waiting. Each dizzying stroke of his body sent her closer to the edge. She closed her eyes, no longer able to hold back the sweet agony that threatened to burst within her. She felt the white-hot flood of passion and gave in to it, abandoning herself to all the mind-boggling delights that came with it. She was barely aware of Edward's own quickened response before he shuddered against her.

Later, still clinging to each other, Edward raised himself and looked into her eyes. "Why didn't you tell me, Maribeth? I never even thought to ask."

"It doesn't matter, Edward," she said softly. "I love you."

He kissed her tenderly. "I love you, too, Gunsmoke." He moved off her and gathered her lovingly into his arms where she curled up like a contented cat. Their lovemaking had made them drowsy, and once again, they drifted off to sleep. Maribeth's last coherent thought was she was going to do anything humanly possible to prevent him from boarding a plane to New York.

Eight

When Edward awoke, the room had grown dim. He glanced at the alarm clock and saw it was almost seven o'clock. Maribeth lay beside him, her slow breathing telling him she was still asleep. Her gold hair curled at her cheek and fell gracefully against her shoulders. He gazed at her and couldn't resist smiling when she made a little sound in her sleep. Lord, he loved her! He moved closer and nuzzled his face against her neck, inhaling the honeysuckle fragrance that was as much a part of her as the air she breathed. She moaned softly and her eyes fluttered open.

"Hi," he said.

She smiled. "Hi, yourself."

"How are you? Are you sore? Can I get you anything?"

"No, but I'd like to use the little girl's room if you don't mind." She started to sit up but realized she wasn't wearing anything. "May I borrow your robe?"

He handed it to her and watched her slip it on modestly and tie the belt securely around her waist. "The . . . uh, washcloths and towels are . . . well, you know where they are," he said, feeling uncomfortable. "Yell if you need anything." She nodded and left the room.

Ten minutes later he was pacing the floor outside the bathroom in his underwear. "Are you okay in there?" he asked anxiously. "Do we need to pull out the ol' first-aid kit or something?" Damn, what a stupid thing to say at a time like this.

Maribeth opened the door and smiled at him, looking much the same as she always had. "I'm okay," she said. She saw the glass of water he was holding. "Is that for me?"

He nodded and handed it to her. "I thought you might be thirsty after . . . well, you know." He was acting like an idiot.

Maribeth took a sip of the water. "I'm really okay, Edward," she assured him. "I'm not likely to die over this, you know. It's *you* I'm worried about, what with your cold and all."

"Oh, I'm fine," he said. "I took one of those eight-hour cold capsules. I still have a good four hours left."

She nodded and made her way into the bedroom, where she began gathering her clothes. "Oh, no, you don't," he said, taking them from her and leading her back toward the bed, despite her protests. He gently eased her on the bed and lay down beside her. "If you think you're just going to have your way with me and leave, forget it."

"Have my way with you?" she said, giving him a lopsided smile.

He rolled over on both elbows and studied her. "Know what I was thinking?" He didn't give her a chance to answer. "I was just thinking how nice it would be if you spent the night here." He saw the doubtful look on her face and hurried on. "I know you have to feed those fat fur balls you call cats, but we can stop by your apartment on the way to the grocery store. I can pick up some steaks and cook them here."

Maribeth considered it for a moment. Her eyes took

in his magnificent body that at the moment was only partially covered. Looking at him made breathing difficult, thinking impossible. Thoughts just disappeared into thin air like puffs of smoke. "Okay," she finally said, "but only if we drop my car off at my apartment. I don't want the neighbors to see it parked here all night. Have you forgotten that Sara Rawlings lives right down the street from you?"

"I couldn't care less about Sara Rawlings."

"Well, I do. She could ruin my reputation in this town forever."

He chuckled. "Nobody has that kind of power, Maribeth."

"You might think it's funny but I don't. I have to live here the rest of my life. You don't."

He arched both brows. "Oh, really?"

"You know what I mean. If things don't work out for you, you can always go back to New York. I don't have anyplace else to go."

"You still don't think I'm going to make it in this town, do you?"

"I didn't say that."

He looked disappointed. "But you have your doubts, right?"

"I just don't want to advertise the fact we're sleeping together."

He relented. "Okay, my little hypocrite. We'll do it your way." He reached for her and pulled her into his arms. "But first, let's take a shower."

Maribeth didn't bat an eyelash. In all of her twenty-four years she had never taken a shower with a man. Not that she hadn't dreamed of it. But she had yet to enter a steamy tiled enclosure with a naked man, and the smug look on Edward's face told her he suspected as much. Well, she wasn't about to give him the pleasure of seeing her cower in modesty, if that's what he expected. She smiled boldly. She could always die of mortification later. "Race you to the bathroom."

Showering with a completely naked man was no small thing, she realized as soon as she had shucked the bathrobe and joined Edward in the glass-enclosed stall. He moved to the back so she could stand directly beneath the warm spray of water. When she was wet, she turned around slowly. He was waiting for her, having already worked up a rich lather in his hands. While she stood there with her heart in her throat, he spread the foamy lather across her breasts, back and forth, drawing circles around her nipples until they became erect. Maribeth blushed in spite of herself. Edward grinned, then leaned forward and nipped one bud with his teeth. When he raised up, he was wearing a soap mustache over his lips. Unable to resist it, Maribeth kissed him and laughed when some of the soap bubbles went up her nose. Edward worked up a fresh lather and spread it across her stomach and thighs. Maribeth felt her heart thump wildly in her chest as his hand slipped between her thighs and very gently washed away the remnants of their lovemaking. His soapy fingers both caressed and soothed her sore muscles as he massaged all pain away. Finally he knelt before her and washed her slender legs and feet. She was overcome with a feeling of tenderness. So strong, yet so gentle.

When he had finished washing her, she took the soap from his hands and held it under the water for a moment. After working up a lather, she spread it across his chest, teasing his nipples much as he had her own. She trailed her soapy fingers down his flat stomach and drew circles around his navel, all the while wondering her next move. When her hands dropped between his thighs to gently soap the intimate region there, she heard his sharp gasp. Nevertheless, she continued washing him, and he responded by growing hard. She could only stare in fascination as she moved her fingers gracefully along the length of him.

"Maribeth." He grasped her hand firmly in his. His features were strained. "If you have any intentions of eating before midnight, I suggest you remove yourself from this shower instantly and let me finish washing."

She blushed to the roots of her hair, already groping for the handle on the door. Edward caught the sight of her shapely hips and couldn't resist caressing them. "Nobody could ever accuse *you* of being shy in the shower, could they?" he said, as she bolted out the door.

Edward was in the process of drying himself when the doorbell rang. He met Maribeth's gaze. "I'll get it," he said, throwing on his robe. "You stay here."

Edward hurried downstairs, wondering who on earth it could be. He opened the door and looked into the face of Moss Gentry.

"Where is she?" Moss demanded, glaring at Edward's robe accusingly.

"Who?" Edward said, being deliberately obtuse.

"Maribeth. Stop playing games, Spears. Her car's outside."

Edward decided it was time to stop the games as well. "In the shower."

Moss's face paled instantly. "So you've bedded her now, huh? Are you proud of yourself, Spears?" He moved closer. "Proud that you stole my girl?"

"I didn't steal her. She was never yours to begin with."

"I ought to take you apart like I wanted to in the first place," he said, his face turning an ugly shade of red.

"Go ahead. That's the only way you know to get what you want," Edward said, his tone harsh. "What are you going to do if Maribeth still refuses to go with you? Beat the hell out of her too?"

"I ain't never laid a hand on her."

"No, you've been more subtle. You've made her feel guilty for not being able to love you the way you want."

"Who the hell do you think you're talking to?" Moss bellowed.

Maribeth, who'd been scrambling into her clothes the minute she heard Moss's voice, dashed down the stairs. "Moss, don't!" She was a second too late. Moss's fist shot straight for Edward's face and made contact with a dull, nauseating thud. She screamed as Edward fell to the floor.

For a second she was too horrified to do anything. Moss dusted his hands together as though he'd just completed a mere task. "He's out cold." Without another word, he turned around and walked out the door.

Maribeth rushed over to Edward, who was already beginning to stir. He held one hand over his eye and managed to raise himself up with her help. "Are you okay, Edward?" she asked.

He grunted and blinked at her. "I think I'm going to be blind in one eye, but other than that . . ."

"Come sit on the couch," she said, guiding him toward it. She helped him sit down. "Oh, Edward. You're going to have one heck of a black eye. I thought you said you knew judo."

He looked hurt as he put his hand back to his eye. "I never saw the punch coming. How am I supposed to defend myself . . . against a . . . a tank, for Pete's sake?"

She sighed. "Well, I better go make you an ice pack."

"I have never been so embarrassed, so humiliated, in my life!" Maribeth said, pushing the grocery cart down the aisle in the store. Edward was right behind her. "People are staring at you."

"They're staring at both of us," he said, "because you haven't stopped yelling at me since we got here."

"Grown men acting like a couple of redneck kids!" she said, stopping in the produce section to pick out a small watermelon.

"I never laid a hand on him," Edward said, trying to defend himself. "What are you getting that for? I hope you don't expect *me* to eat any of it."

"Of course, I do. All southerners eat watermelon."

"I'm not a southerner."

"Oh, Lord, there's Martha Hines. Turn around so she doesn't see you. She'll think you're even more of a fool. Oh, darn, she spotted us."

"Edward!" Martha hurried over to him. "What in heaven's name happened to your eye?"

"Moss beat him up," Maribeth said, surprised at Martha's concern.

"He didn't beat me up," Edward said, offended.

Martha pursed her lips together in irritation. "That Moss has always been a big bully." She reached up and touched the area just under his eye. "Oh, my, that's going to be a real shiner. Have you done anything for it?"

"I put ice on it."

"Well, if it doesn't get better, I'd call Doc Henderson. He makes house calls, you know. By the way, I got the job."

"Good for you!" he said, and waved as she started down the aisle.

Maribeth was dumbfounded. "Since when have you and Martha become such good friends?"

He shrugged. "I guess she had a change of heart."

"You've been covering her checks, haven't you?"

"Are we going to talk bank business or buy groceries?"

Maribeth gave him a funny look. "You know, sometimes I think I know you well; other times I don't think I know you at all."

• • •

"Why don't you make the salad and I'll put the potatoes in the oven to bake?" Edward suggested after
they'd returned to his house and unloaded the groceries. "You *do* know how to make a salad, don't you?"

"I'm not totally incompetent in the kitchen," she said
coolly.

"That's all right. You make up for it in the bedroom."
Edward didn't have to look at her to know she was
blushing. Once he'd washed, pricked, and oiled the
potatoes, he put them in a pan and into the oven.
Then he leaned on the counter and watched her finish
the salad. Her hands fascinated him. They were slender and delicate with long beautifully tapered fingers.
He already knew what those fingers could do to him.

She looked up and saw a question in his eyes. "Is
something wrong?"

"I don't know. I'm a little overdue on this, but, well, I
didn't know how to ask you earlier."

She arched both brows. "Ask me what?"

He was uncomfortable. He'd never had to ask a woman
in his life. But then, none of the women he'd known
were like Maribeth. "Are you . . . uh, taking anything?
You know. For protection?"

She stared at him for a full minute before his meaning sunk in. "Oh, that." She laughed self-consciously.
"Well, actually, when I knew we might . . . you know, I
got a prescription for birth-control pills. And speaking of
pills," she added briskly, "don't you think it's time you
took your cold medicine?" She handed him the bottle.

He shook his head as he went to the sink for a glass
of water. "Oh, Maribeth," he said. "I never know what
to expect from you." He popped one of the cold capsules in his mouth and watched her. "I suppose that's
why I fell in love with you." He moved behind her and
slipped his arms around her waist. "You make me feel

ten feet tall when I'm with you." He nipped an earlobe playfully, and she shivered. "Let's make love again."

Her stomach gave a sudden lurch at the husky sound of his voice, and she laid her knife down, dried her hands on a towel, and turned around in his arms. It was like coming home, a feeling so strong, it made her heart swell in her chest. She rested her head against his shoulder.

He slipped one finger beneath her chin and raised her face so that he was looking into her soft eyes. The look there mirrored his own feelings. "Sweet, adorable Maribeth," he whispered before taking her lips in a kiss that left them breathless and aching for more.

Maribeth felt her body grow weak as Edward's lips moved over hers expertly, as his tongue slipped into her mouth and mated with her own. The kiss deepened, and he drew her closer and closer against his hard body as though he were trying to pull her inside of him. He smelled of soap, the same soap she had lovingly used on his body earlier. She could still picture him as he looked then—lean and brown and hairy, with white lather running down his wide chest and flat stomach. She leaned into the embrace, offering her lips freely. She was his for the taking. His lips traveled down her throat and up to one ear, and she trembled with delight. Feeling more comfortable with him now, she slipped her hands beneath his shirt and massaged the taut muscles of his chest, running her fingers through the crisp curls. She could lose herself with this man. He surprised her by lifting her high in his arms. She wrapped her own arms around his neck and kissed him as he climbed the stairs to the bedroom.

Their lovemaking was slow and leisurely. Edward's hands were painstakingly thorough as he touched and caressed her flesh, which under the light from the hall, was the color of ripe peaches. Her skin tingled as his lips rained soft kisses across her breasts, along the valley between them, and over her flat stomach. When he entered her, he was again cautious, afraid of bringing her pain. She sighed and slipped her arms around his waist and pulled him even closer. They peaked at the same instant, then slowly floated back to reality, their bodies entwined. Afterward they merely lay together, embracing and listening to each other's heartbeat.

At last Maribeth stretched and sighed. "I've never made love with a man who had a black eye."

He chuckled. "And I've never made love to a woman who shoots bank robbers."

She raised up on one elbow and gave him a look of pure indignation. "This is the last time I'm going to tell you, Edward. I did *not* shoot the man!"

By the time Edward carried in two medium-rare steaks, Maribeth was ravenous. They both did justice to their dinner, despite the fact they were unable to keep their eyes off each other. "You look like a thug," she said, giving him a slip of a smile. "I feel like I'm having dinner with Al Capone." She frowned. "What are you going to do tomorrow? You have to go to work in the morning, you know."

He shrugged. "I guess I'll have to go in looking like a thug, huh?"

After cleaning the kitchen, they curled up in Edward's bed, only after he absolutely refused to let Maribeth wear the cotton gown she'd brought. Maribeth, who'd never slept nude in her life, found it wasn't so bad after all. She lay in the crook of his arm and sighed in sheer pleasure as he stroked her hair. Edward only half listened to the program on the television set as he held her close. This was so right, so perfect; what he'd always been looking for. He climbed out of bed only

STRAIGHT SHOOTIN' LADY • 151

long enough to switch off the TV then rejoined Maribeth beneath the covers. They fell asleep in each other's arms as the first gentle roll of thunder sounded in the distance.

The shrill ringing of the telephone jolted them awake sometime later. Blinking in the darkness, Maribeth could barely make out Edward's lean form as he fumbled for the telephone on the bedside table. He mumbled something into the receiver and waited as the person on the other end spoke. When he hung up he was wide-awake.

"What is it?" Maribeth asked, her heart beating erratically from the sudden awakening.

Edward rubbed his eyes, already rising from the bed. "Hector Billings's barn was struck by lightning," he said, feeling for the light switch. "It's burning. They need my help." He flipped on the switch and reached for his clothes.

"But why did they call you?"

"Some man offered me a job as a volunteer fireman at the Chamber of Commerce meeting. Didn't I tell you?" He stuck his legs into his jeans.

"We weren't speaking at the time," she said, springing off the bed, her eyes darting around the room for her own clothes. "I'm going with you."

"No, it might be dangerous."

"I don't care. I want to go. Besides, you don't even know where Hector lives."

"He lives a couple of blocks from the Community Club," he said, fumbling with the fastening of his jeans. "I should be able to spot a burning building."

"I'll worry about you," she said. "If you don't take me, I'll hitch a ride with someone else."

He glared at her. "Dammit, Maribeth—" He stopped when he saw the frightened look in her eyes. "Oh, all right. But you'll stay in the car. I don't want to have to fight a fire and worry about you at the same time. Is that clear?"

"Yes, Edward."

They were on their way in minutes. A fine mist of rain was coating the roads, making driving hazardous, and Edward was not able to go as fast as he wanted. Maribeth pointed the way. "It's just around that bend," she said. They both stared wordlessly at the sky; a strange glow was hovering over the trees. "It must be bad," she said grimly.

What they saw when they rounded the last curve made them both gasp. "Good Lord!" Edward said. The rafters, as well as most of the midsection of the barn was aflame. The fire was out of control.

Edward parked his car as close as he dared. Men raced back and forth across the yard, carrying hoses and shovels and other tools. Two antique looking fire trucks were parked at a respectful distance. "Stay here," Edward said, and jumped out of the car. He ran toward the barn and patted one man on the back. "What can I do?" he yelled over the roar of the fire.

The man's face was covered with soot. "Relieve one of the others. You'll find extra gear in the trucks. It's too late to save the barn. We're just trying to keep the fire from spreading to the woods." He glanced over Edward's shoulder at Maribeth. "You can help Hector try to round up some of his livestock that got away."

Edward swung around and saw her. "I thought I told you—"

"I have to help Hector," she said, and ran in another direction.

Several hours later Hector's barn lay in a shambles. Only a few pieces of charred lumber stood against a purple sky; everything else was soot. The predawn air smelled of smoke and ash. Maribeth stared at the scene, depressed and exhausted.

"Are you ready to leave?" Edward asked her, looking just as tired.

Hector came up to them and slipped his hand in Edward's for a handshake. "Thanks for coming," he said. The creases in his skin were caked with soot, and he looked ten years older. His blue cap was scorched.

Edward returned the handshake. "Let me know if there's anything I can do."

Hector nodded and attempted to smile. "You need to take care of that eye, son."

Maribeth had fallen asleep by the time they reached Edward's house. The sky was a soft pink, the sun only minutes from rising. Edward helped her into the house, and they showered quickly, trying to scrub away as much soot and grim as they could before falling into bed.

Maribeth arose at eight and dressed for work, despite Edward's protests. "You need your rest," he said. "I can take care of things at the bank." She refused to listen.

If anyone at the bank noticed Edward's eye, which Maribeth was sure they did, they were polite enough not to mention it. By eleven o'clock she was dragging and wished she had taken Edward's advice and stayed in bed. He wasn't much better. His cold had worsened in the night air, and he looked awful. She was in the process of pouring herself another cup of black coffee when Hector walked through the door.

"Got another one of those?" he asked, pointing to the cup.

"Hector!" She quickly poured him a cup and handed it to him. "This is a nice surprise."

"Good morning, Hector," Edward said, coming out of his office and extending his hand. The older man took it and shook it. "Got a minute?" he said. "I'd like to see you in your office if I could."

"Certainly." Edward stepped back and motioned for Hector to pass through first. He and Maribeth exchanged curious glances. It was a well-known fact that Hector Billings had no use for banks. "Please hold my calls."

Maribeth was prevented from pondering the whole thing when a teller called her out front to help a customer who was having problems. By the time she returned to her office, Hector was on his way out. He was frowning. "Everything okay?" she asked, giving him a hopeful smile.

"Just dandy," he said in a voice that suggested otherwise. He tipped his scorched cap and lumbered out the door.

Maribeth hurried into Edward's office, where she found him slumped in his chair, twirling a pencil, looking mournful. "What's wrong with Hector?" she asked. "He looked mad enough to tear open our vault with his teeth."

Edward tossed the pencil onto his desk. "He wanted to borrow seven thousand dollars to rebuild his barn and replenish his livestock. I turned him down."

"You did what?"

Edward stood and shoved his hands into his pockets. "The man can't repay the loan, Maribeth. He's on Social Security and it barely feeds him. How's he going to pay back the money?"

"Do you realize what you've done?" she said incredulously. "You refused to loan money to Hector Billings, the very backbone of this community. Why, Hector built this town. He's responsible for what it is today."

"Don't you think I know that?" Edward said, sounding as miserable as he felt. He raked his hands through his hair. He had hoped she would understand his decision. "What am I supposed to do, loan money to people merely because they're well liked in the community and to hell with the fact they can't repay the bank?"

"Hector would have paid it back," she said loudly.

"He *can't* pay it back," Edward said just as loudly. "He doesn't have the funds."

"You sure sound like a New York banker," she said spitefully. "All you care about are your figures and percentages and your precious computer printouts. You don't give a hoot about the people you're supposed to be serving."

"That's not true," he said angrily. "I offered to loan Hector the money personally, and he wouldn't agree to it."

"I could have told you that," she said. She threw her hands up in frustration. "You've ruined everything. All we've worked for."

"Maribeth—"

"What do you think people are going to do when they find out you refused to loan money to Hector? I'll tell you what they're going to do. They're going to jerk every cent they have out of this bank."

His jaw was hard. "You're exaggerating again."

"Oh, you think so? You still don't understand these people, do you? I spent much of my childhood on Hector Billings's knee listening to ghost stories. So did half this town." She sighed. "I can't go on working here—"

"That's enough, Maribeth."

She ignored him. "You don't belong here, Edward," she said, tears burning her eyes. "Moss was right all along. You're an outsider. Why don't you go back where you belong? I thought we had a chance, but I was wrong."

Edward slammed his fist on the desk. "That's enough!" he yelled. "Has it ever occurred to you I might have other ideas on how to help Hector? You still don't have enough faith in me, after all we've been through." He took a deep breath, trying to calm himself. He felt rotten; physically and mentally rotten. And she was about to walk out on him again as she had before. "I'm sorry you feel as you do about us," he said, his voice a bit calmer. "I knew we had our differences, but I thought we could work them out. If you want to quit your job, that's up to you. At least I'll know once and for all where we stand. But I can't and won't make business decisions based on your personal feelings." He turned around and walked back to his chair and sat down. "Now, if you'll excuse me, I have a lot of telephone calls to make."

Maribeth walked out of his office and closed the door behind her. Tears blurred her eyes as she grabbed her purse from her desk and left.

Nine

Maribeth went job hunting the following day. Only a handful of jobs were posted in the *Gazette:* a waitress position at the J&M Restaurant, a convenience-store clerk, and an assistant librarian at the local library.

"The job doesn't pay much," Doris Bagby, the head librarian told her. "But we give a salary increase every year."

Maribeth tried to compute mentally what she would bring home every two weeks. It would be barely enough to pay her rent and buy groceries. "I'll take it," she said, realizing it could be months before she found anything more suitable. "When can I start?"

By the end of the week Maribeth was beginning to wonder if she'd made a mistake. Although there was plenty of work at the library to keep her busy, there was absolutely no one to talk to. Doris stayed bottled up in her office—a glass-enclosed room, the only room other than the bathroom where one could speak without whispering. The head librarian's cool demeanor did not invite conversation. Maribeth missed the little talks she'd had with Edward. She missed Edward period. Perhaps she should have taken the waitress job, she thought, climbing into her car late Friday afternoon when she got off work. She'd splurged and purchased a new battery because she knew Doris would not tolerate tardiness as Edward had.

Carol called that evening. "Edward needs you, Maribeth," she said. "The place has been a zoo all week without you."

"Did he *say* he needed me?" she asked, balancing the telephone on her shoulder as she tried to open a can of cat food. She had already slipped into her gown, having decided to go to bed early and forget her troubles. Edward had not so much as tried to telephone her. Not that she had expected him to.

"All his plants are dying, Maribeth," Carol said, as though that in itself were proof enough.

"His plants were dying before I left." Maribeth sighed. "I know you mean well, Carol, but I can't come back. There are just too many problems. We don't get along. We're too . . . different."

"I think you're just being stubborn, Maribeth," Carol said, heaving a sigh of frustration. "Dan was right. I should stay out of it."

Maribeth hung up a few minutes later, only after swearing to Carol she would be all right. She climbed into bed and snapped off the light, determined not to lose another night's sleep over Edward Spears. But it was useless. She hadn't slept well all week. Why should tonight be any different? Why hadn't he called?

It was obvious, she told herself. He hadn't called because he was fed up. "I never know if you're for me or against me," he had said. The truth hurt. She had not had enough faith in him. She had walked out on him, not once, but twice; both times when he needed her most. Tears filled her eyes, but she didn't bother to wipe them away.

• • •

On Sunday Maribeth had dinner with her parents—stuffed cornish hens and sweet-potato soufflé, her favorite. It could have been sawdust for all she cared.

"What's wrong with you?" her father demanded. "Your mother went to all this trouble, and you've hardly eaten a thing. You look as miserable as a dairy cow with sore teats."

"Now, Frank," Effie said, "that's no way to be talking at the dinner table." She gave Maribeth a sympathetic smile. "Maribeth's probably just having her monthly. You know how I used to get."

"Her monthly?" he said as though he hadn't heard her right. "You tell me I can't talk about a cow's teats at the table and here you are talking about—" He and his wife began to argue.

Maribeth had been relieved when it was time for her to leave. She spent the rest of the day doing laundry and cleaning her apartment. Several times she picked up her phone to make sure it was working right. Face it, she told herself, slamming it down, Edward is not going to call. It was finished, over, terminated.

On Monday she returned to the library, determined to throw herself into her work and forget ever laying eyes on the man. Doris's aloof manner didn't change. So that's why she's an old maid, Maribeth thought. The week seemed to creep by for Maribeth. The only relief was her lunch hour, which she often spent with Carol, eating their sandwiches in the square. It was an unspoken agreement they wouldn't talk about Edward.

"My, but your disposition has grown sour," Carol said on Friday. "Do you realize you haven't smiled all week?"

Maribeth couldn't help but laugh. "I know. My cats are threatening to move out. I don't know why you put up with me."

"Because you remind me of Edward. He doesn't smile either."

At the mention of his name Maribeth stood up. "Well, I'd better get back before Doris Bagby comes looking for me. Have a nice weekend." She hurried away.

Maribeth frowned in her sleep when the persistent knocking didn't go away. Doris Bagby's image floated before her. Was she late for work? No, it was Saturday. Or was it? She wasn't sure anymore. Her tears had left her exhausted and confused. She wasn't sure of anything except how painful it was when she awoke and thought of Edward. She slid deeper under the covers. Sleep was her only escape. Nobody was going to steal it from her.

Maribeth came wide-awake when the knocking grew louder and threatened to rouse the whole neighborhood as well. She fumbled for the alarm clock and groaned. Five-thirty in the morning. Someone was either crazy or desperate. She froze. Her parents. Had something happened? She sprang into action, kicking off the bedcovers as both cats mewed in protest. She didn't even think to put on a robe. Frantically she groped her way toward the kitchen, stopping only long enough to pull a large rolling pin from one of the kitchen drawers. Just in case. More knocking. She reached for the outside light switch and flipped it on. She peered through the curtain on her back door and gasped in surprise. Standing on the other side of the door, holding one large grocery sack with another at his feet, was Edward. She merely stared for a moment, feeling as though the breath had just been knocked out of her.

She turned on the inside light, slid the chain free, and unlocked the dead bolts, still clutching the rolling pin in her hand.

"You're not going to hit me with that, are you?" he asked, as he picked up the sack.

"Uh, no." She laid the rolling pin on the counter. "What's going on?"

"I need your help," he said, coming through the doorway and setting the bags down. He began unloading packages of meats and cheese. "I need you to help me pack enough lunches for about two dozen men. I—" He turned and looked at her and his words died in his throat. He swallowed hard as he took in the tight fitting T-shirt and wispy panties she wore. A band of flesh peeked out at him where the hem of her shirt didn't quite meet the elastic waistband of her underwear. Her legs were as long and slender as he remembered. Her hair was tousled beguilingly, her skin flushed from sleep. His gut wrenched with desire. "After you get dressed," he said, a bit harsher than he'd planned.

Although she was mortified with the fact she was wearing very little, she glared at him for having the audacity to say anything. "I'm sorry if my appearance offends you, Edward," she said, mustering up as much dignity as she could under the circumstances, "but I don't receive many callers at this hour." She folded her arms over her breasts, hoping to conceal her nipples, which she knew were straining against the flimsy fabric of her shirt. Just let the man walk in the room, and her body went ape on her. She was angry now. Who did he think he was anyway, barging into her place like this? He hadn't so much as called, and she had cried enough tears to fill one of those grocery sacks. She gritted her teeth.

"Maribeth—"

"How dare you walk into my apartment in the middle of the night and order me around! Just who do you think you are? And why in the name of heaven do you need that many sandwiches anyway?" She had to pause long enough to catch her breath.

It was Edward's turn to get mad. It was obvious as hell she wasn't happy to see him. Just because he'd spent a miserable two weeks thinking about her didn't mean she had done the same. He had picked up the telephone a dozen times to call her, but had hung up. Their problems couldn't be solved with a simple phone call. He'd made a mistake in coming, that much was certain. "The food is for the men who are going to build Hector's new barn," he said, tossing the sandwich meat and cheese back into the sacks. He would make them himself.

Maribeth dropped her arms to her side in disbelief. "Well, why didn't you say so?"

He looked up in surprise. "Then you'll help?"

"Of course, I'll help," she said. "As soon as I'm dressed," she added in a snippy tone.

Hector Billings padded barefoot from his bedroom into the kitchen, muttering hotly under his breath that someone should choose to bang on his back door before seven o'clock on a Saturday morning. He threw the door open, ready to give whoever it was the tongue-lashing of a lifetime. He blinked in surprise when he looked into Maribeth's face. "What's wrong?" he asked quickly.

Maribeth thought Hector looked strange without his cap. "Good morning, Hector," she said as though he hadn't spoken. "Got any coffee?"

He frowned. "I reckon I do. But ain't it kinda early for you to be out visitin'?"

"Not when there's so much work to do," she said matter-of-factly, ignoring the steadily growing noise behind her. "I need coffee for about twenty-five men. Think you can manage that? You could always pull out the urn we use at the Community Club meetings."

Hector rubbed his eyes. "Maribeth, what in tarnation is going on?" he demanded.

"Why don't you come out on the back porch and see for yourself?"

Both brows drawn together in a fierce frown, Hector followed her out onto the back porch in his paisley pajamas. He gaped at the scene before him, and she couldn't blame him. His backyard looked like a parking lot. A steady stream of cars, trucks, and campers were pulling into his driveway. Among them was a flatbed truck piled high with new lumber. "What's that?" he asked, his confusion mounting.

Maribeth smiled. "Lumber. For your new barn."

Hector stared at her for a moment, shocked. "Where'd the money come from?"

"The Community Club donated the money in appreciation of fifteen years hard work."

"Then you can tell 'em to turn around and take it all back," he said, turning back for the kitchen door. "That money is for the park."

"The park is already paid for," Maribeth said. She stopped him before he went in. "One of our members went to visit Mr. Burns, thinking if he was kind enough to donate the lot for the park in the first place, he might help us finance the project as well. Mr. Burns, surprisingly enough, offered to pay for the whole thing, including the playground equipment. He said it was the least he could do since the Community Club had made so many improvements to the town." She grinned and leaned closer to Hector. "And we both know old man Burns can afford it."

Hector couldn't stop himself from grinning with her. "He always has had more money than brains." Then he sobered. "But I can't accept this kind of gift, Maribeth."

Maribeth saw that his eyes were watering. "You *have* to accept it, Hector," she said vehemently. "Think how hurt everybody would be if you turned it down." She knew now why Edward had sent her to give the man the news. He had suspected Hector would try to refuse. "Please take it," she said softly, reaching out to touch his arm. "You know how much we love you."

Hector stared past her where the men were already at work, unloading the telephone poles that would support the barn. There were six of them on the truck, enough to build a good size barn. "Whose idea was this?" he asked, a lone tear sliding down his cheek.

"I think you know the answer to that." Maribeth gazed across the yard and found Edward, already hard at work, picking up burnt and charred pieces of Hector's barn. She wished they could pick up the pieces of their relationship, but knew it was unlikely. It was obvious Edward had come to realize, as she had, it could never work. He hadn't said a handful of words to her on the drive out.

Hector chuckled under his breath. "Crazy New Yorker. I reckon I owe him an apology. And a whole lot more," he added. He looked at Maribeth. "What do you want me to do?"

Maribeth tried not to let him see how close to tears she was. "First I want you to get dressed," she said, a little too brightly, "and get out of those awful pajamas. Hector, I do declare those are the *ugliest* pajamas I've ever seen. Too bad they weren't in the barn the night it burned." She shook her head. "Then start making coffee. We're going to need gallons of it." Hector was grinning as he made his way into the house.

By lunchtime six telephone poles stood partially buried in the ground, with adjoining boards nailed at the top and bottom, making a large rectangle that would serve as the foundation for the barn. While some of the men worked with the tractor and bore, digging holes for the barn, the others built the rafters that would be raised to the very top of the new structure with large pulleys. Maribeth watched in fascination as she and

Carol and some of the wives carried lemonade to the men. When they weren't doing that, they picked up small debris from the fire and loaded it into cardboard boxes to be carried to the dump. Maribeth found herself looking up often from her work in search of Edward. Although she knew he had never built a barn in his life, he seemed to be pulling his weight more than adequately. He had removed his shirt, just as many of the other men had, and she couldn't seem to keep her eyes off his broad back and chest.

"Don't you think it's time we started passing out lunches?" Carol suggested, wiping sweat from her brow. The weather had turned warm after an unseasonable cold front. Maribeth wasn't listening. Carol followed the direction of her gaze. "And don't you think it's time you two made up?"

Maribeth blushed, realizing Carol had caught her gawking at Edward. "I've already told you, Carol. It's over."

"I know what you said. The two of you are just too different, right?" When Maribeth nodded, Carol went on. "You know something, Maribeth. I think you have to be one of the stubbornest people I've ever met. You never give an inch, do you? And look at Edward. He's done everything humanly possible to build a life for himself here. Why, he wears those boots everywhere he goes, and we both know they hurt his feet."

"I know," Maribeth said. "Believe me, I've done nothing else but think about it for the past two weeks. And now that I realize it, it's too late." She felt close to tears. "I refused to believe in the man, Carol. Even though he promised me he would make a place for himself here. I was scared to take a chance. I let him down, Carol. And I don't think I'll ever be able to forgive myself for it."

Carol started to say more but didn't. "Come on," she said, slinging her arm over Maribeth's shoulders. "Some of the women have already started passing out lunch sacks. You and I can hand out the cold drinks. By the way, did you know there's going to be free barbecue at Jake's Tavern for everybody afterward?"

Maribeth worked as hard as the men for the rest of the afternoon. Edward effectively ignored her, or at least that was how it seemed. When the rafters went up, amid shouts and whistles, he was on the other side of the barn talking to Moss, of all people. The last ray of sunlight had faded by the time the final boards were nailed into place. A couple of men planned to return the following day to do the finishing work, but as it stood, the barn was ready for use. As the men began packing away their tools Hector stared at the barn in awe. It was bigger and nicer than the one he'd lost. He cried.

"Who licked the red off your lollipop?" Moss asked, coming to stand beside Maribeth.

"Don't start on me, Moss. I'm not in the mood."

"Oh? Must be catching. Lover boy's mood is about as sour as cow's milk after she's been in the onion patch. You want me to give you a ride to Jake's?"

She nodded. "I would appreciate it."

As they rode to the tavern, Moss was strangely quiet. When they got there, they found Jake and several other men shoving tables together to accommodate everybody while Jake's wife stood behind the bar filling mugs of draft beer. Jake joined her and began carrying them to the table. No one thought anything when he disappeared in back for a few minutes, but when he returned, he headed straight for Edward. He placed an open bottle of beer in front of him.

"What's this?" Edward asked, glancing up at Jake in surprise.

Jake crossed his arms over his big chest. "That's the fancy beer you asked for, ain't it?" When Edward nodded, Jake grinned and slapped him on the back. "I can't have my customers driving to the next town for a cold beer now, can I?" He winked. "There's more in the cooler."

Maribeth stared in stunned silence. When Edward looked her way, their eyes met and locked. Something passed between them, an emotion so strong, it made Maribeth's stomach flutter uncontrollably. She was the first to look away. She sipped her beer and ate barbecue like the rest of the group, but her mind was on Edward, as always.

Toward the end of the meal Hector stood and banged a knife against his beer mug until the group fell silent. He removed his cap. "I want to make sure I get a chance to thank everyone before you all go home," he said. He glanced around the table and smiled. But when he started to speak again, his look was serious. "I don't recollect a time when anybody has done something this nice for me." He paused. "I couldn't have made it without that barn. As you know, most of my livestock has been rounded up. . . . Some of you here have been nice enough to board the animals for me until I could take care of them again. I appreciate that." He reached for his beer and took a sip, and it was obvious he was trying to get his emotions under control before he continued. "The person I'd especially like to thank is Edward Spears, for organizing this whole thing." He gave Edward a genuine smile and Edward smiled back. "Mr. Spears has already done more for this town than most folks who've lived here all their lives." He grinned. "Anybody who was at the fair knows the beating he took in the dunking booth." The group laughed as a look of distaste crossed Edward's face.

"Hector, would you get to the point so I can serve another round of beer?" Jake taunted from the bar, and the whole group burst into laughter. Anyone who had ever attended a Community Club meeting knew Hector had a tendency to drag out his speeches.

Hector laughed good-naturedly and waved him off. "What I'm trying to say is"—he looked at Edward—"we appreciate all you've done and hope you decide to make this your permanent home. I would like to personally nominate you for our next treasurer when the Community Club meets again." Hector sat down.

The group clapped loudly for Edward, Maribeth included, her eyes filled with tears. She smiled at him proudly. Whatever their differences, Edward had worked hard to achieve his goal of gaining the town's respect. His bank would succeed.

Edward stood, surprised, and a bit embarrassed with all the attention. He'd only meant to help Hector out after his stroke of bad luck. He'd never expected this. "Hector—" he paused and cleared his throat—"that's the nicest thing anybody has ever said to me," he said, giving the man a warm smile. He glanced around the table, then back to Hector. "I appreciate your proving your confidence in me by asking me to run for treasurer of your fine club, but"—he hesitated for a moment—"unfortunately, I won't be in town for the next meeting." A couple of people shook their heads in disappointment. "I have to fly to New York in a couple of days on business. However," he said when a murmur went through the group, "I will have someone running the bank in my absence, so business will go on as usual." He gave them a sincere smile. "But I truly appreciate the offer just the same." He sat down as the people applauded.

Maribeth's smile was frozen on her face. She wished the floor would open up and swallow her. "Do you want to leave?" Moss asked her.

She nodded thankfully. When she stood, her legs felt like putty. Somehow she managed to say her good-byes to everybody, the smile still plastered to her lips. She followed Moss out the door, tears already streaming down her face.

"Where do you want to go?" Moss asked, helping her into his truck.

"I don't care. Just drive until I stop crying."

Moss jumped in and started the truck.

"Listen," Maribeth," he said twenty minutes later. "You're either going to have to stop crying, or I'm going to have to go to a gas station. I've burned up half a tank of gas already, and you've probably lost two quarts of body fluid."

"And I've run out of tissues," she said, wiping her red nose. Moss drove a few more miles, then pulled off the road. "Are we out of gas?" she asked.

"No. I just want to talk to you." He parked and shut off the motor, then sighed. "Maribeth, I want you to go to that Spears fellow and work things out betwixt the two of you."

She stared at him openmouthed. "Have you flipped your lid? Last week you almost knocked his head off because we . . . because . . . well, you know. . . ."

"That was before I realized how much he loved you. And you love him." Moss's expression was resigned when he looked at her. "I've fought a lot of battles in my life, Maribeth, but I always knew when to walk away from one. I'm going to walk away from this one because I've already lost. That man is in love with you, Maribeth. Now, you're going to have to face up to the fact that you ain't getting any younger. And you won't find many men who are going to put up with that sharp tongue of yours. As I see it, you'd better jump on this chance before it's too late. He wants to marry you, you know."

Maribeth looked at him in surprise. "Did he *say* he wanted to marry me?" she demanded. "I mean, did he use the word *marriage*?"

"He did." Moss shrugged. " 'Course, that was this

afternoon, before he told us all he was going back to New York. He could have changed his mind."

"Changed his mind!" she shrieked. "He can't change his mind on such an important issue just like that," she said, snapping her fingers. "What do you think I should do?"

"I cain't tell you that," he said. "You started making your own decisions a long time ago."

"Then let's go straight to his house," she said. "If Edward said he wanted to marry me, then I'm holding him to it." Moss cranked the engine and pulled back onto the road. When they had driven a mile or so, Maribeth looked up at him. "What are you going to do?" she asked softly.

He shrugged. "Drive trucks, I reckon."

"No, I mean personally."

"Don't worry about me, Maribeth. I'll get by. I always do."

Maribeth decided not to press him. Moss had a good way of looking after himself. She talked about nonessential matters as he drove to Edward's, realizing she was becoming more nervous the closer they got. Moss turned down Edward's street and pulled into his driveway. His Mercedes was parked there and the lights were on in the house. "I guess he's here," she said, wiping her sweaty palms on her jeans.

"Yeah, it looks like it."

"What if he has changed his mind, Moss?" she asked, losing some of her former zeal.

"That's a risk you'll have to take."

Maribeth felt her eyes fill with tears once again and realized she had cried more that day than she'd ever cried in her life. She hugged Moss. "I'll never stop loving you," she said with a sob, "and I'll never forget the good times."

"Me neither," he said thickly. "Now, get out of here." He pointed a finger toward the house like an angry parent sending his child to bed. When she climbed out and closed the door, he grinned. "I'm sure you can think of some way to keep him here."

Maribeth turned around and walked slowly up the sidewalk toward Edward's house. Behind her, she heard Moss pull out of the driveway and start down the street. She stopped at Edward's front door and took a deep breath, trying to get a grip on herself. What if Edward had changed his mind about wanting to marry her? A marriage proposal wasn't valid unless both parties were present, was it? She stood at the door for several minutes before she worked up the nerve to ring the bell. She was going to give it to him straight, tell him exactly how she felt. And she was *not* going to let him run off to New York and leave her brokenhearted.

Edward opened the door. She opened her mouth to speak, then clamped it shut when she saw he was wearing only a towel. She hadn't counted on that. Concentration would be difficult. He looked more than a little surprised to see her. "I have to talk to you," she said bluntly, determined to keep her eyes above his shoulders.

He backed away from the door and motioned for her to come in. His hair was wet from the shower he'd just taken, and droplets of water stood out on his shoulders and chest. "What is it?" he asked. One hand was gripping the knot on the towel.

She faced him squarely. "Edward, I can't let you go to New York," she blurted out, not knowing any other way to say it. "I want you to stay in Laurel and marry me like you told Moss you wanted to." She paused. "You *did* tell Moss you wanted to marry me, didn't you?" she asked hopefully.

"News travels fast in this town," he said. He folded his arms on his chest and studied her for a moment. "I did," he admitted, "but that was before I got to thinking about all those things you said, like I didn't belong here and I would never understand these people and we didn't have a chance because we were too different." He paused. "Need I go on?"

So he was going to rub her nose in it, make her grovel. She took a step closer, trying not to stare at his broad chest as she spoke. "Edward, you don't have to change one smidgen for me," she said adamantly. "I love you just the way you are. This town loves you. Why, I figure by the time the Chitterling Strut rolls around, you'll be like a regular member of the family." She was avoiding the real issue, and she knew it. Her eyes misted over.

"Edward, you have every right to hate me for walking out on you those times you needed me most. You don't know what it's been like living with that. I'm so ashamed."

"And so you should be," he said.

She sighed. "But I love you, Edward, and I'm willing to work on these things so we can have a good relationship. I'll work like a horse if I have to." She slipped her arms around his waist because she couldn't help herself. She gave him a funny half-smile. "But if you don't do the honorable thing and marry me like you already said you would, I'll have daddy hunt you down like a dog and—"

Edward laughed and pulled her tight against him. He put his hands on either side of her face and gazed tenderly into her eyes. "I don't think you'll have to resort to that." He kissed her gently.

Maribeth fell limply against him. When he broke the kiss, she clung to his shoulders to keep from falling. "Then ask me right now, Edward," she said hoarsely, "so I'll be able to hold my head up in this town.

He considered it for a moment. "Bossy to the end, aren't we, Gunsmoke?"

She stared in stupefaction. "Well, you certainly don't expect *me* to do the proposing, do you? Why, if Sara

Rawlings ever caught wind of that, folks would never stop laughing at me behind my back."

"Okay," Edward muttered. He made a big production of getting a throw pillow off the couch and tossing it to the floor. Again grasping his towel with one hand, he got down on one knee. "Maribeth Bradford," he said, "would you do me the supreme honor of becoming my wife?"

The smile she gave him was as brilliant as sunlight. "Yes," she said.

"Wait a minute, I'm not finished."

She waited, folding her hands primly in front of her.

"And would you promise to love me and stop trying to boss me around?"

She sighed.

"I'm waiting for your answer."

"Yes," she said between clenched teeth.

"And watch that mouth of yours?"

She tapped her shoe on the floor impatiently. "Yes! Anything else?"

He gave her a self-satisfied smile. "I think that about does it."

She squealed in delight and threw her arms around him. He lost his balance and they both toppled to the floor laughing. His towel came loose. The laughter died instantly as they gazed at each other in sheer adoration. "Oh, Edward," she said, breathlessly. The love and desire she felt for him was so intense, it frightened her.

He carried her upstairs to the bedroom, his eyes never leaving hers. "I think it's time I showed you some of the things I'll be expecting of you once you become my wife," he said, his voice thick with emotion. The look in her eyes mirrored his own feelings. Never had a woman been able to touch all his emotions like Maribeth. She could make him happy enough to sing and mad enough to chomp steel. And she could make him feel like a million bucks. He laid her on the bed, his hands already working frantically at the buttons of her blouse.

Maribeth gazed at his body, already feeling the desire build in the pit of her stomach. She caressed his thigh. It was hard and feathered with the same dark hair that covered the rest of his body. "What exactly *are* you going to expect of me?" she asked coyly.

"Well . . ." He paused and pulled her shirttail out of her jeans. "First, I expect you to stop talking back to me." He arched one brow, but there was a glint of amusement in his eyes. "I suppose you'll have to work on that one, huh?" He slipped the blouse off her shoulders and tossed it aside. A second later her lacy bra followed. When she was bare from the waist up, he merely gazed at her, worshipping her with his eyes. "I love you, Maribeth," he whispered. When he fastened his lips onto one nipple, she crooned in pleasure.

Maribeth ran her hands lightly over his chest, tracing the hard muscles with a fingertip and drawing tiny circles around his nipples until they were taut. When Edward claimed her lips, she let her fingers trail down his stomach to his navel and below, where he was already growing hard with need. She filled her palm with his maleness and wondered if there would ever come a time when she would touch him without feeling awed. Probably not. She began stroking him gently, deriving much pleasure out of the simple act until he groaned and took her hand in his. "It's been too long, Maribeth," he said, answering the question in her eyes. "I love you touching me like that, but . . ." He let the sentence trail off as he brushed her lips with his own before moving back to her breasts.

She held his head with both hands as he suckled. When he began nipping her gently with his teeth, she felt a strong tug in the pit of her stomach that sent a delightful feeling of warmth between her thighs. "Oh,

Edward," she whispered breathlessly, pulling his face closer.

"Do you like that, sweetheart?"

"Y-yes!"

He paused and looked into her passion-glazed eyes. "There's so many things I want to do to you, love. So many wonderful things." He concentrated once more on her breasts, until she began to squirm beneath him. She arched her hips, and he knew she was ready for him, but instead of answering that need with his hardness, he trailed his lips down her stomach, past her navel and beyond. He felt her stiffen and become still. "It's okay, sweet," he said tenderly, looking into a pair of bewildered eyes. "Just relax." He stroked her thighs open wide so that he was looking at her feminine beauty with open adoration. Once again he worshipped her with his lips.

Maribeth gazed down at him through a film of desire. When he found the very center of her passion, she grasped the covers tightly and bit her bottom lip to keep from crying out. Her mind reeled at the wonderfully wicked things he was doing to her. She fell back on her pillow, thinking she would surely lose her mind. She closed her eyes and felt her hips begin to move of their own volition. Suddenly her eyes flew open. "Edward, I think I'm—"

"Go ahead and give into it, love," he said. "Don't hold back."

He didn't have to coax her further. All at once her body took over, and all rational thinking ceased. A surge of passion flooded her and made her cry out. Edward continued loving her, even as her passion subsided. In seconds, though, she felt another rise and gave into it, her eyes filling with tears at the sweet release. Edward raised up, loving the way she stared at him in amazement. He kissed away the tears. He was hard and ready for her. He entered her cautiously and

moaned with sheer pleasure as her body grasped him
tightly. For a moment he just lay there, too caught up
in the moment to do anything but gaze into her lovely
eyes. Then he began to thrust gently, his forehead
perspiring as he forced himself to remain controlled.
"Tell me how it feels, love. Tell me."

Maribeth found herself being caught up in the sensuous game of words. "You feel so good, Edward. So
good . . . so wonderful."

"Wrap your legs around me, Maribeth," he ordered,
his breath hot on her cheek. "Yes, that's it. Oh
Maribeth. . . ."

They made love fiercely, having been too long without each other. Edward's lips were everywhere, hot on
her flesh. Before long Maribeth found herself aching
for relief once more. Edward whispered words in her
ear that sent her into a wild abandonment. Their cli-
max was urgent and frenzied, each crying words of love
and adoration and pleasure. When their passion was
spent, they clung together, feeling their hearts pound
in their chests and listening to their own labored
breathing.

Maribeth grinned up at him. "Nobody could accuse
you of being shy under the covers, could they?"

Edward chuckled, moving off her and pulling her
into his arms. He slowly floated back to reality, and his
look grew pensive. "Maribeth?" He pulled her tighter
against him.

"Mmm?" She had not come back to earth yet. A
funny smile outlined her lips, one of pure feminine
satisfaction.

"Did you and Moss talk?" He knew the time probably
wasn't right for a serious discussion, but he wanted to
get some things straight between them.

"Yes."

"And?"

"We're friends again."

He grinned. "So when are you going to take me to meet your parents?"

"Is tomorrow too soon?"

He chuckled. "Tomorrow sounds fine. Do you think they'll like me?"

She shrugged. "It might be uncomfortable at first. Mama and Daddy are just two simple people, Edward. Daddy is a bit gruff at times, kind of like Jake, I suppose, but he's a wonderful father. As long as I love you, that'll be good enough for them." She snuggled closer. Edward's warmth enveloped her like a soft glove. "You make me so happy. Were you as miserable these past two weeks as I was?"

"More."

A comfortable silence fell over them as they held each other, basking in the afterglow of their lovemaking. Finally Maribeth raised up on one elbow. "Edward, I know we've never talked about it, but I hope you want children, because I do." She saw him smile and nod. "But where will we raise them?" she asked as an afterthought. "We can't very well raise children on white carpet and vanilla furniture that looks like it came straight out of Hugh Hefner's mansion. Think what it would look like eventually."

He chuckled. While she was talking about something off in the future, he was dying to make love to her all over again. Would he ever get enough of her? He doubted it. "Okay, we'll change it," he said, looking up at her worried expression. He began stroking one breast and watched in satisfaction as the nipple contracted eagerly. They were so right for each other. "We'll put in indoor-outdoor carpeting and buy all our furniture at garage sales. Will that make you happy?"

She laughed and buried her face against his chest. "I'm going to make you so happy, Edward," she said fervently. "I know you think my ways are a bit strange at times but—"

"I think you're wonderful." He put a finger beneath her chin and raised her head so she was looking directly into his eyes. "I know we're different people, Maribeth, but that's what makes it so much fun. We'll never get bored with each other." He grinned. "I don't care if you handle a gun like Matt Dillon. And did I tell you I bought a Waylon Jennings tape the other day?"

She was tempted to tell him she'd checked out *Moby Dick* at the library, but she was going to wait and see if she could make it through the first chapter. A thought hit her. "But why were you going back to New York?"

"I'm still going back to New York," he said. "Like I said, I have some business to attend to. For one thing I have a buyer for my condo. I plan to tie up all my loose ends there. I want to live in this town permanently, Maribeth." He smiled. "I've come to love this place and the people who live here." He saw the expression of surprise on her face. "Did you ever doubt it?"

"Maybe just a little," she said meekly.

"And I want you to come to New York with me," he said. "It'll give you a chance to meet my parents." A worried look entered her eyes. "Don't worry, they're going to love you as much as I do. And you have to meet Hildegarde." He grinned. "You're going to love Hildegarde."

"Uh-huh," she said skeptically, then laughed.

"While we're there, we can discuss wedding plans. I think we should be married right away."

"I'd like to be married in the little country church here, Edward. I've known Reverend MacPhee all my life. He'd be sorely disappointed if he couldn't marry us. Do you think your parents could fly down?"

"I'm sure they would."

With all the talk of going to New York and planning her wedding, Maribeth forgot about something. "What about my job at the library?"

He was silent for a moment. "I don't want to make

demands on you, Maribeth, but I would prefer you gave it up. I need you at the bank."

"You mean, you want me back?" she asked in disbelief.

"Of course, I do. I never wanted you to quit in the first place." He gave her a sexy smile. "Unless you'd rather stay home and start making babies right away. But the job is yours if you want it."

She sighed. "Okay, Edward," she said in a tone that suggested she was about to make the supreme sacrifice. "I'll quit my job at the library." Secretly she was relieved. But she wasn't about to tell him that. She might need it for bargaining power in the future. "I'll come back to work at the bank. And keep my opinions to myself," she added.

He frowned. "I never said I wanted you to do that, Maribeth. You're . . . uh, outspokenness was one of the first things that attracted me to you." He moved his hand to her other breast and stroked it lightly. "Your opinions are important to me. But you're going to have to face the fact we may not always agree with one another. I think I'm a fair-minded person, but if I make a decision at the bank that you don't personally agree with, you're going to have to have enough faith in me that I'm doing it for the good of the bank." He grinned. "You can always hit me over the head with that rolling pin once we get home."

She wound her arms around his neck. "I don't want to fight with you, Edward," she said. "Most things just aren't worth it. I believe the only thing worth fighting for is our love. And I *do* have faith in you, Edward. I know I was slow coming around, but you did just as you promised, you made a place for yourself here." She pulled him close for a kiss.

"Wait a second," he said, breaking the kiss. "I forgot to show you something." He climbed out of bed, unabashed in his nakedness, and hurried in the direction of the bathroom. He was back a few seconds later carrying a large cardboard box.

"What is it?" Maribeth asked, sitting up. He put the box on the bed and she cried in delight. "A puppy!" She reached into the box and pulled out a squirming, round-bellied puppy with a deep golden coat.

"It's a golden retriever," Edward said proudly. "I saw him advertised in the *Gazette* and bought him."

Maribeth snuggled against the grunting pup. "Oh, but why are you keeping him in the box?"

Edward frowned. "He's not exactly potty-trained."

"What are you going to do with him while you're in New York?"

"Hector offered to look after him. I don't suppose he'd mind looking after those overweight cats of yours as well."

She gave him a dirty look. "They're not overweight, they're . . . uh, plump. Besides, I can always ask my parents to take care of them." She looked back at the puppy and smiled into a pair of sleepy brown eyes. "Besides, it doesn't look like this little fellow has ever missed a meal," she said, rubbing his round belly. "What's his name?"

Edward laughed. "So far I've been calling him damn dog. He has his days and nights mixed up. He wants to sleep during the day and play at night."

Maribeth gave him a seductive smile. "That doesn't sound like such a bad idea to me."

Edward placed the dog back in the box and set the box on the floor. "I've seen enough of that dog for now," he said. "All I want to look at is you."

He kissed her, his tongue sliding teasingly in and out of her mouth. He pushed her gently on the bed and slipped his hands around her, his arousal growing with each breath he took. Suddenly he raised his head. "By the way, what's a chit-ling? Is it like that godawful stuff you call fatback or salt pork, that stuff everybody around here seasons their food with?"

"Make love to me again, Edward," she whispered, nuzzling her lips against his neck.

"Because if it is, I'm not going to eat any. A man can only do so much, you know. I still have blisters on my feet from wearing those boots."

"I love you, Edward," she said tenderly. "Just the way you are."

"I love you too, Gunsmoke." And captured her lips in another kiss.

THE EDITOR'S CORNER

I AM DELIGHTED TO WELCOME KATE HARTSON AS YOUR AUTHOR OF THIS MONTH'S EDITOR'S CORNER, AND TO LET YOU KNOW THAT NORA ROBERTS'S NEXT SIZZLING ROMANTIC SUSPENSE NOVEL—**SACRED SINS**—WILL COME OUT NEXT MONTH.

HAPPY HOLIDAYS!

Carolyn Nichols

I'm delighted to have joined the LOVESWEPT team as Senior Editor to work on these fabulous romances, and I'm glad to be writing the Editor's Corner this month so that I can say *hi* to all of you.

Isn't it a treat having six LOVESWEPT books every month? We never have to be without a LOVESWEPT in the bedroom, den, or purse. And now there are enough of these luscious stories to last through the month!

Soon we'll be rushing into the holiday season, full of sharing and good cheer. We have some special LOVESWEPT books to share—our holiday gifts to you!

RAINBOW RYDER, LOVESWEPT #222, by Linda Hampton, is a gift of excitement, as our respectable heroine, Kathryn Elizabeth Asbury, a pillar of the community, finds herself attracted to Ryder Malone, a wildly handsome rogue who has a penchant for riding motorcycles. Kathryn's orderly life is shaken by Ryder, who isn't quite what he appears to be. She fights hard for control

(continued)

but really can't resist this wild and free-spirited "King of the Road." Then she makes a thrilling discovery—and falling hard doesn't hurt a bit. **RAINBOW RYDER** is sure to be one of your favorites, but don't stop reading, we have five more LOVESWEPT GIFTS for you. . . .

Diamonds are the gift in Glenna McReynolds's **THIEVES IN THE NIGHT,** LOVESWEPT #223—how appropriate for the holiday season! Our heroine, Chantal Cochard, is an ex-jewel thief forced out of retirement when her family's prize diamond necklace shows up around some other woman's neck. DIAMONDS may be a girl's best friend, but they're not her lover. That's better left to well-built, sexy men like our hero, Jaz Peterson. Once Chantal invites him into her Aspen hideaway, she quickly learns that love is the most precious jewel of all!

Witty Linda Cajio's gift to us is **DOUBLE DEALING,** LOVESWEPT #224, a story of childhood dreams and adult surrender. Our heroine, Rae Varkely, mistress of a fabulous estate, is forced into a position where she simply has to kidnap Jed Waters. She makes a ransom demand, but our hero refuses to be released! Making demands of his own, he turns the tables on Rae, who can't help but pay with her heart. Still she has to protect her property from Jed's plans for development. But Jed has no intention of destroying anything—he only wants to build a strong relationship with the mistress of the manor.

A new book from Kay Hooper is always a gift, but **ZACH'S LAW,** LOVESWEPT #225, is an especially wonderful one. As the tale continues of those incredible men who work for Joshua Logan (and who indirectly fall out of SERENA'S WEB), we meet petite Teddy Tyler stranded on a deserted mountain road. Zach Steele, a strong, silent type who frightens Teddy because he ignites such strong desire in her, is her rescuer . . . then her sweet jailer . . . and the captive of her love. But Hagen's got his claws into Zach, there's mayhem on the horizon, and there's Zach's own past to confront before true love can win out!

(continued)

Sara Orwig's **OUT OF A MIST**, LOVESWEPT #226, is a gift of desire, as Millie and Ken are reunited after a brief but unforgettable encounter. Ken is on the run from the law, and Millie discovers him wounded and hiding in her closet. Of course, she knows he's done nothing wrong and she lets him stay with her until they can clear his name. But the longer he stays, the more he finds a place in her heart. Millie blossoms in Ken's embrace, but Ken won't settle for just passion—his desire is the lasting kind!

Our final romantic gift for you is a wonderful new book by Patt Buchiester called **TWO ROADS**, LOVESWEPT #227. This moving book is a story of healing: Nicole Piccolo is recovering from a broken leg and a broken heart, trying to forget Clay Masters, the man who promised her *forever* and then disappeared from her life. When Clay reappears a year later, the wounds are opened again, but Clay is determined to show Nicole that he never meant to leave and his heart has always been hers. When the healing is complete, they begin again with no pain to mar the exquisite pleasure of being in love.

Enjoy our gifts to you, sent with love and good cheer from your LOVESWEPT authors and editors!

Kate Hartson

Kate Hartson
  Editor
LOVESWEPT
Bantam Books, Inc.
666 Fifth Avenue
New York, NY 10103

The first Delaney trilogy

Heirs to a great dynasty, the Delaney brothers were united by blood, united by devotion to their rugged land . . . and known far and wide as

THE SHAMROCK TRINITY

Bantam's bestselling LOVESWEPT romance line built its reputation on quality and innovation. Now, a remarkable and unique event in romance publishing comes from the same source: THE SHAMROCK TRINITY, three daringly original novels written by three of the most successful women's romance writers today. Kay Hooper, Iris Johansen, and Fayrene Preston have created a trio of books that are dynamite love stories bursting with strong, fascinating male and female characters, deeply sensual love scenes, the humor for which LOVESWEPT is famous, and a deliciously fresh approach to romance writing.

THE SHAMROCK TRINITY—Burke, York, and Rafe: Powerful men . . . rakes and charmers . . . they needed only love to make their lives complete.

☐ *RAFE, THE MAVERICK* by Kay Hooper

Rafe Delaney was a heartbreaker whose ebony eyes held laughing devils and whose lilting voice could charm any lady—or any horse—until a stallion named Diablo left him in the dust. It took Maggie O'Riley to work her magic on the impossible horse . . . and on his bold owner. Maggie's grace and strength made Rafe yearn to share the raw beauty of his land with her, to teach her the exquisite pleasure of yielding to the heat inside her. Maggie was stirred by Rafe's passion, but would his reputation and her ambition keep their kindred spirits apart?   (21846 • $2.75)

LOVESWEPT

☐ YORK, THE RENEGADE by Iris Johansen

Some men were made to fight dragons, Sierra Smith thought when she first met York Delaney. The rebel brother had roamed the world for years before calling the rough mining town of Hell's Bluff home. Now, the spirited young woman who'd penetrated this renegade's paradise had awakened a savage and tender possessiveness in York: something he never expected to find in himself. Sierra had known loneliness and isolation too—enough to realize that York's restlessness had only to do with finding a place to belong. Could she convince him that love was such a place, that the refuge he'd always sought was in her arms?

(21847 • $2.75)

☐ BURKE, THE KINGPIN by Fayrene Preston

Cara Winston appeared as a fantasy, racing on horseback to catch the day's last light—her silver hair glistening, her dress the color of the Arizona sunset . . . and Burke Delaney wanted her. She was on his horse, on his land: she would have to belong to him too. But Cara was quicksilver, impossible to hold, a wild creature whose scent was midnight flowers and sweet grass. Burke had always taken what he wanted, by willing it or fighting for it; Cara cherished her freedom and refused to believe his love would last. Could he make her see he'd captured her to have and hold forever?

(21848 • $2.75)